About the Author

Tancredi Lyle Rapone is a young adult of the 21st century. And he would like you to read a story which is partially autobiographical, but at heart larger than his own life. It is a perception of the tendencies of a generation which, he feels, lives in between disparagement towards the past and boredom towards the future.

He would like the twenty-first century to be remembered as an epic quest for strength spurred by the apparent lack of domineering will which surrounds us all.

Tancredi Rapone

THE HUMAN GOD

AUSTIN MACAULEY
PUBLISHERS LTD.

A CIP catalogue record for this title is available from the British Library.

ISBN 9781786123695 (Paperback)
ISBN 9781786123701 (Hardback)
ISBN 9781786123718 (E-Book)

www.austinmacauley.com

First Published (2016)
Austin Macauley Publishers Ltd.
25 Canada Square
Canary Wharf
London
E14 5LQ

"Man is a God when he dreams,
A beggar when he reflects"

Friedrich Hölderlin

Preface

It is common knowledge, that *it's the things we don't choose, that make us who we are,* family, neighborhood, heritage...

This may very well be true, but if so,

Where do we draw the line between what we cannot choose and what we, *don't* choose?

It's always during the first years of our lives that we make the choices which will determine our destiny. And only through the cataphracted "Illumination of youth", what most people label as an emotional turmoil of adolescence, can we refuse the parts of society which ultimately set us off course, and discover our true selves.

And we forge our legacy.

Tancredi Lyle Rapone

"At bottom every man knows well enough that he is a unique being, only once on this earth; and by no extraordinary chance will such a marvelously picturesque piece of diversity in unity as he is, ever be put together a second time."

Friedrich Nietzsche

The days pass, time as the dimension of the world, the measure of life. And my life stays still. And I sit, on the edge of the void, as the vortex spins out of control, above my head. I can catch a glimpse of the exit, one step beyond transcendence, with my youth expiring in the time dimension.

Ever since I've existed in this world, I've always found great difficulty in finding excitement in my life, and a meaning of my *piously human* surroundings. The simple distinction of the days, the hardest task I was set, and the identity of the creator of the task, the greatest mystery I was to uncover.

My existence depended on the influence of ideals and idols, which had no reference to me, and helped me survive in a world I did not belong to.

I sought guidance, but the kind of guidance I could not find in the tangible world, which quickly spiraled beyond contempt.

In a desperately goliardic search, I started imagining different versions of my life, nuancing its aspects and *characters* to the different circumstances of reality, and, sometimes, even more than that.

As I grew, I found a word to define my condition: cataphraction. Its ambiguous meaning, polyvalent in infinite ways. Literally, a form of protection, a soldier with a full-body armor, cataphracted in face of the battle. And the greatest of all predicaments, was not to be the fear of death, but the uncertainty as to the origin of his strength, either the same fear surging from the image of the battle, or the transcendence of his spirit.

I was never a soldier, or much of anything else, but I theorized and imagined myself as a warrior going through life. The battle, always consisted in not falling into anonymity, the vortex of my surroundings. The armor, which shielded me against the pain of frailty and spiritual weakness; alcohol, cigarettes, and the otherwise pitiful existence, by *ordinary* standards, at least a guarantee of keeping me different and distant from a society which terrorized me.

Slowly, this alteration degenerated, and reality and imagination merged into, a field of potential reality, or, with a more dangerous denomination, the *cataphracted world*. And I found a somewhat, excuse the expression, *more realistic* representation of myself, and the ambience of my condition.

While I kept on living within my imagination, on the outside, I was fighting a war against everything and everyone, including myself.

But the pain which ensued, was necessary, and the cataphraction eventually surpassed, the transcendent meaning of it all, finally uncovered.

My name is Max; I am the author of this book. Either the delusional and melancholic visions, of a raging alcoholic, or a prophet, an original thinker, and a symbolized and truly idyllic version of the *human God*. Capable of creating his own *faithful* reality, as he makes no distinction between the tangible world and the transcendent voyage undertaken in his mind, ravaging through the spatial-temporal dimension. And his greatest ability of all, is not that he can create by building, he creates by selecting and eliminating his pain, negating the aspects of his society which have been miscontrived and lost along the way.

The ability to impose the cataphracted world upon the world he lives in.

I give you my account of the painful ordeal, which has been my life —that is if indeed I ever existed...

Chapter 1

The Vision

I woke up at around eleven am. The sunlight came in the window, seeping through the venetian blinds, and set itself on my eyelids. By the time I had managed to lift my head, my neck muscles gave up, sending it crashing back down onto the pillow. I wondered what I would do with the day, and whether I would manage to make it any different from the day before, and the ones before that.

She came out of the bathroom barely dressed. And made her way, carelessly, through the piles of books that cluttered my apartment. Just another anonymous face in my life. We went through the trivial morning-after routine. With every word spoken I felt as if I lost a crumb of integrity from my heart. The heart I had followed with reverence when I was younger. Or maybe I hadn't. It was too long ago to remember and my memory had been losing pieces for a while, and I had stopped caring somewhere in-between. I got up, forcing myself to stand straight and keep my composure, regardless of the hangover that was sullenly banging on my head. We had breakfast on the terrace and smoked a cigarette. Few words were said and the awkwardness in the air must have been terrible. But I was too tired of it all to feel awkward, so I ignored her nervous chitchat, nodding and approving once in a while. And closed my eyes, letting the sunlight bless my face.

She was pretty. In the moments when the sunlight shaded the right parts of her face, you could still catch a glimpse of that young beauty which you knew had once dazzled and mesmerized every young man it crossed. She had blonde hair and innocent eyes. Those features, which had once been young and pure, were now puffed up and twisted by plastic surgery.

We got dressed, I put on a pair of beige pants, a white shirt and a blue suit jacket. She was wearing the same black cocktail dress she had on the night before and a raincoat. Her back was exposed for a brief moment, before she flung the coat over her shoulders, and I caught a glimpse of the horrid tattoo at the base of her spine. For an instant, I was dazed in the remembrance of a girl I had once loved, and lost. Along with everything else.

I thought of taking an umbrella, since the weather was a bit uncertain. But I decided against it, after all, it was getting warmer as the winter faded and made way for the spring. When she was ready to go, I opened the door for her, and closed it behind me with a thud. Stepping out of the building, I set foot on the soil of the old town of Rome, my only true home. We walked past all the antiquarians on Via Margutta, the fashion stores on Via del Balbuino, and finally got to the taxi stand on the near side of Piazza Del Popolo. We said a hasty goodbye and she got into the cab, all too quickly. I handed the driver fifty euros and told him to take her wherever she wanted to go, he could keep the change. That was it, there was no "thanks for last night", or "I'd like to see you again, sometime". As the driver started the engine, she suddenly changed her mind and reached for my hand. She looked at me and forced a pitiful smile.

"You will keep in touch won't you?" It was a very strange thing for her to say, as if I were leaving for a very long trip, or something were changing in the status of a non-existing relationship. I grinned

"Certainly," I said, my *manners* prevailing upon sincerity.

I knew that was the last time I would ever see her. And I was glad of it.

As I stood there, the Piazza was flooded with the noise coming from the cafes, where regular people were starting their day; and the traditional Sunday morning routine was on display as the tranquil Italian way of life. Not able to resist the temptation of idleness, I thought it would be a good idea to commence on the right foot and have breakfast. Just then my phone started ringing. It was my good friend Martin, he had just gotten up and wanted to have a champions' breakfast with me.

The "champions'" breakfast, was an invention of mine and my friends'. It consisted in a Negroni Sbagliato and a coffee. Over the years we had dropped the coffee and stuck to the booze, although that wasn't the only thing we'd dropped. With time people started dropping out, as they moved on with their lives, and left us behind. The only ones left in the group were myself and Martin.

The Negroni Sbagliato is a typical Italian cocktail, based on Campari, dark vermouth and Spumante, which is champagne produced in Italy.

I met him at the *Canova Tadolini*, the old study of the homonymous 19th century sculptor, which had now been turned into an exclusive bar. It was on Via del Balbuino, about halfway between Piazza del Popolo and Piazza di Spagna, that the magnificently blasphemous bar stood, as the world past in front of it, indolent to its cultural value. I went inside and made my way, navigating through the hundreds of marble sculptures which crowded the room, to a small table at the back.

Martin was spot on time as always. He was wearing a brown suit and an old trench coat. He took off his hat when he came through the entrance, and nodded politely, first at the owner, then at me. He came towards the table, walking his presence out of the twenties. As usual, his appearance was a perfect preview of the man beneath it... such a cliché

Even though he had never been very successful in his academic career, he was extremely cultured. His general knowledge came from an ocean of books he read periodically. What I couldn't understand about his reading habits, notwithstanding the numerous conversations we had on the topic, was that he never, under any circumstance, read a new book. In his mansion of an apartment, there could not have been fewer than a thousand books, all of which he had read, or so he said, before he turned twenty. Then he stopped reading entirely for a long time, before reconciling himself with his library and reading every single book over, and over again. If there was something in the world I could ever know, I'd like to know, of all the books he had, which one was the last new one he had read.

Anyways, he never failed in cordially monopolizing conversations on any subject which might have come up at the gatherings of the Roman upper class. He was the sort of person that everybody listens to when they're talking. His words were as if carved in stone, his tone was slow and precise, he was always in control of everything. Few times had I seen him lose an argument, or, in general, change his opinion. And he never went back on his word. His actions were always perfectly coherent with the things he said, and the people he respected. Of all the friends and acquaintances I had, Martin was truly the only one I had always emulated and admired. His elegance, the intriguing paradox, of the emblematic society he pertained to.

Through all the years I had known him, I had never seen him lose his temper, or behave in an ungentlemanly way. I looked up to him, and saw him as my guide through the madness of our lives.

His physical appearance was pleasantly average, he had dark hair, medium height and medium build.

We ordered our drinks and got the usual queer look from the waiter. Ignoring him, we started making small talk as he reluctantly got to work. We quickly went through weather and gossip.

"Oh Martin... Where did it go?" I said in a depressed tone, shaking my head.

"What do you mean?"

"What happened, to us? What happened to our ideals and our goals?"

"Nothing changed, Max."

"So much time..." I said, thinking of how long I had been living in that beautiful town doing nothing. His expression became more serious, as he realized what I was referring to.

"It's all lost.

"Still though, what would you have done with it?"

"I wanted to change something, to be someone. To leave a legacy.

"The more I keep living this life and the more I realize I'd like to go back to the beginning."

The waiter brought us our drinks. He gently set them down on the table and left quietly. The bar was more than half empty on a Sunday morning. I could only catch a glimpse, through the statues, of a few people sitting at another table. They were in their sixties. He had red hair, stylishly gelled back, and was older than her, perhaps near to being seventy. She had blonde hair, and was wearing a red dress and was quite loud. I heard the echo of her voice, through all the statues. A very uneven, yet familiar, background ambience. We didn't talk for a while, and for some reason, I found myself thinking of the couple behind the statues. In my twisted mind I lacked any form of parental guidance. So all I saw, were the idyllic statues in the way; between myself and a connection to a model, superior to the idols and more similar to me.

Then I remembered how alive this bar used to be, and now it was dying; along with the usual faces of the people I knew, which had now been substituted by others. Their only difference residing in that ineluctable youth I had been envying since I'd turned thirty-five. But as they would get older, they would attempt to make excuses for keeping that reprehensible lifestyle. They would cover themselves with lies, inside and outside. Killing the soul, and the pleasant memories, they had once lived with.

Martin did not to fall in this hypocrisy, that's why I respected him. He embraced his reality, rather than living in denial. He was destined to fail, nonetheless he truly did love his own peremptory self.

He finally collected his thoughts, looked into my eyes, and said:

"It may sound fake, or corny, but the truth is; life is a one chance game. You cannot go backwards, and you can only choose your direction in life, not much else. We're all going to die in the mud, Max. But as long as we're living here we must do something valuable with our lives, we must do what we were meant to accomplish, not for society or legacy, but because we owe it to ourselves.

"Now, we don't all have to want the same things, but on the matter of accomplishment and life changing choices we must be absolutely certain. Just make sure you're not chasing something abstract enough to set you off course." – He paused and looked at his drink, before leaning back in his chair and, defenselessly, resuming his monologue, unsatisfied by his own statement.

"You know, we're part of the same vortex, you and I; we spend our lives spinning our wheels and doing nothing. Rather than chasing something, and covering your true self with remorse, embrace it. It's the only way you can prepare for the day you're finally ready to get out."

He broke sight and took a long drink. I raised my own elbow and said,

"What do you want from life?"

He smiled at the question and leaned forwards, easing the tension.

"Have fun, drink the finest wines, love the most beautiful women, drive an old car, read good books, write great ones, but most of all, be surrounded by the best and happiest friends," His answer was so sure of itself and quick, it almost seemed rehearsed, as if he were afraid of being challenged.

We're not happy, I thought to myself. But I only managed to say,

"That's what we've been doing for years."

"So, what more should you want?" he replied grinning.

"You know just the other day, I was walking around town. It was around lunch time and I passed in front of a school. And I saw these kids, Martin, these kids, with their piercings and tattoos, taking pictures of themselves, as if they were editing their lives. They looked so lost. Just a feeling I had passing in front of them.

"If I could help only one of them to find himself and change his life. My legacy would carry on."

I don't know why I said that. I think I regretted it even before I spoke. But the meaning of my clench to those pious words, somehow became more evident throughout my life. It was not the words themselves, but the desperate quest for humanity symbolized beneath them, that cluttered my mind.

Martin concentrated, hanging on it all, and said,

"Remember when we were that age?"

"Yes."

We painfully chuckled and shook our heads, simultaneously taking a sip from our drinks.

"Look, do you want my advice?" he said, changing the subject – "Write another book."

"When I wrote *that* book I was inspired. Look around, where am I going to get the inspiration now?

"Besides 'Our problem' (my first book) was never as good as it should have been. Perhaps, in the end, I didn't have much else to say."

"You're a very talented writer, Max."

"I've lost faith in writing, Martin."

"You can't say that; I won't allow it." The sudden change of tone in the conversation surprised me. I looked at him and he looked at me, maintaining his statement and waiting for the question.

"Why not?" I said. I was tired of being preached to, even from him.

Quickly, he answered with a phrase which was not his own.

"Because the difference between what we read and what we write is the only proof we exist."

It was something I had said over twenty years before and had never said again. The memory of how much faith I used to have in the world and in myself was painful. I looked at my drink, ashamed, and looked back at Martin. There was no self-irony or apprehensiveness in the way we looked at each other.

We wore the most expressionless faces ever seen on the face of the earth, but in that brief moment of intimacy, I thanked him. Friendship wasn't the word, to describe what kept Martin and me together. To euphemize, we were coercively bound by the world which we had fallen into, involuntarily, and helped each other in a codependent relationship. A.K.A. Fu---ed.

"You know, your 'humble' productions aren't half bad either," I offered, getting off the topic of my book and my life as a writer. It always bothered me when people spoke to me as a writer, since I had never really felt like one. I guess it was just another costume I wore once in a while to masque the brutal uncertainty which ruled my life.

"I'm a historian, I wrote historical reports, you can only *be* so original. I did something many people could do," he said. Just then his phone buzzed, he slightly raised his hand in sign of apology, and looked at it.

"I've got to go, family matter. I'll see you around."

He raised his finger signaling for the bill, I quickly and subtly shook mine. I would never have allowed him to pay. He just said, "Thanks, old boy," and left.

I sat there for a while, thinking of the conversation we had just had, and trying to find something helpful in Martin's words. I wondered if maybe I should start writing again. When I was younger I had dreams of entering the banking sector or maybe opening my own financial services firm. I wanted to lead my life in a radical way, and do something my parents would never have approved of. But in the end, what difference did it make *to me*, I was filthy rich, who wanted to be *radical*. Still, everyone needs an occupation in life, and in my case I use the term loosely, so I decided to manage the various fortunes of some of Rome's wealthiest families. Well, in some way, I had realized my juvenile dream, but it wasn't really the same. Who was I kidding? These people hadn't hired me for my qualifications, actually I didn't have many. They had hired me because they trusted me. All they wanted were stable, safe investments which could allow them to maintain their extravagant properties and continue living in the Renaissance. So where did that leave me? I was just the man who dealt with their "business", doing my best to keep them away from the 'Guardia di Finanza', the Italian tax police.

I looked at my watch and decided I should probably drop by the office. It was entirely unnecessary, but at least it gave me something to do. I left some cash on the table, and finished my drink.

In those days, my abundant consumption of alcohol gave balance to my dissatisfaction with life, protecting me from my fear of death, the human predicament *par excellence*. It would be useful to elaborate more on this particular aspect of my *cataphraction*. But the truth is there isn't much to say, except I did not see it as a means of escaping my reality. It was more of a filter to my life, something that allowed me to blend with my problems and subdue the pain which inevitably surged.

On my way out I crossed the owner, he offered to buy me a drink, but I politely declined. As I walked down the grey sidewalks of Via del Balbuino, on that wonderfully sunny day, I wondered what Martin's family problem could have been. He didn't have much of a family, really. His parents split up when he was very young, his mother left the country and remarried. He lived with his father for a while, until the tension got to be too much. Finally, when his father moved out and left him alone at age sixteen, he was only relieved. They never had gotten along anyway.

My story was similar to his, I had never really gotten close to my parents either.

I spent the rest of the day at the office, searching for investments that met the unusual requirements of my clients. After my quotidian wrestling match with the disadvantages of having an infinitely boring job, I had dinner at the "Vecchia Roma" with Giorgio Altemps, the major shareholder of the fund. We discussed the new tactics to screw the tax police in front of a wonderful meal. I laughed at the thought that the Guardia di Finanza probably had the place under surveillance. It was their latest trick: they inspected the registers of high end restaurants and checked the tax returns of the clients. If a person, apparently on welfare, ate in a five-star restaurant, they knew something wasn't quite right. Giorgio asked me why I was laughing, so I told him. He chuckled and said he had booked under my name. I shook my head and laughed, again, at my sly friend.

In the end, I decided it wasn't worth it to try and give him a speech on ethics and the evils of tax fraud, so I just cautioned him against breaking the law. Giorgio and I went way back; we had agreed to disagree a long time ago. Still, more than my client he was my friend. When we were kids we had talked about going into business together, doing what, we had no idea; but the difference in our views had always instilled mutual respect. Though I wasn't too sure I could still claim to believe in the things I did when I was younger. Over time it becomes more and more difficult, to sustain a belief without actually doing something in its respect.

When we finished our four-course dinner, Giorgio insisted on paying the bill. I invited him for dinner at my place the next week and we said goodnight. I thought about getting a cab, but after all, I only lived 20 minutes away, and it was such a nice evening, so I decided to walk home, reminiscing the youthful memories the city had left me. I crept out of the back streets of the Roman city center and entered Piazza Venezia. The huge square was dimly lit by the moonlight, and the old malfunctioning streetlights. The Vittoriano, what tourists call the "wedding cake" and communists call "the typewriter", towered over the city. The monument dedicated to the Unknown Soldier and to the first king of Italy, was perhaps one of my favorites in Rome. The white marble gave a sense of peace, whereas the classical structure and the enormous proportions inspired freedom war, and the power of Rome in modern times. Standing there, in front of the greatness, I intimately felt there wasn't a single soul who shared my admiration. And my consternation in front of the fall from the idols, to the mundanely tangible world around.

I walked in silence down Via del Corso, passing through my old neighborhood. Every street corner had a story to it, some better than others. When I passed by the St Charles church I saw a bunch of people gathered outside. They were all piously huddled together, as they stood on the steps of the extravagantly baroque church. Their black suits collectively formed a cloud of darkness, splashed onto the white marble. The fact they were all uniformed in their grievance attire, coercively indicated they must have been *celebrating* a special occasion. Besides, no one ever attended the late-night masses anyway, only old people and lost sinners.

Out of curiosity I guess, I got a little closer and blended into the group. Notwithstanding the closed casket, abandoned upon the altar, there was a pitiful lack of emotion. Only one person was crying, he couldn't have been older than twenty. He was wearing a midnight blue suit, shirt untucked, either out of weariness, or reverence to a plebeian fashion trend. His blonde hair was all over the place, was it going up, down, sideways, I don't know. He was fairly tall, maybe a little shorter than myself. He didn't really look like he fit in with the rest of the group, his watery eyes were filled with anger and hate. He looked at me, and I nonchalantly deferred from eye contact. This must have upset him. For a brief, but painful second, he waved a closed fist at me and appeared on the verge of throwing a fit. Suddenly, a man came out of the crowd, walking in his pedantically elegant posture, Martin. He approached the boy and put both hands on his shoulders. Martin said something in his ear, then the boy said something and Martin just nodded, understandingly. Martin handed the boy his coat, since it was fairly cold and he was wearing a lightweight suit. When he finished comforting him, he came towards me, somehow having already seen me even before he laid his eyes on my zoned body. He didn't seem particularly enthused.

"Hey, what are you doing here?" he said in a confident manner, not at all surprised.

"I..." I paused trying to think of something to say.

"I was just passing through, I should go," I said, raising my hand.

"Come on, let's go get a beer."

"Are you sure? I can see you're busy."

"Don't worry about it, I could use an excuse to get out of here," he said under his breath, slapping my shoulder in a friendly manner. He said a few politely hasty goodbyes, and exited the baroque church and reached into his pocket for a cigarette. I followed only a few steps behind. He fumbled, searching for his lighter, which was probably in one of the pockets of the coat he had left with the boy. I got my gold zippo out and lit it for him. He nodded in sign of appreciation, took a long puff from his cigarette, and blew the grey smoke into the cold night. I lit one myself and we walked down Via del Corso towards Piazza del Popolo. The street was empty. All the tacky department stores and what was left of the smaller boutiques, which during the day were filled with people, were now closed. I felt at ease. We remained in silence, and didn't look at each other.

When we got to Piazza del Popolo, we stood there and looked at the huge obelisk. Behind it you could see the doors enclosing the old city. Still, no words.

Martin took one last puff from his cigarette and flicked it, magically landing it in a garbage can.

"Lowenhaus?" he said.

"Sure,"

The Lowenhaus was a trendy pub near my place. It fell on a side street that connected Via del Corso to Via del Balbuino. Via Margutta, my street, ran parallel to Via del Balbuino.

"Old memories hu?" I said.

"Some better than others," he replied, smiling and slightly tilting his head towards the ground.

We got to the pub, sat outside and ordered some beers.

We had danced around it for a while now.

"I won't ask if you don't want me to," I said.

"Do you remember my father, Max?"

I was surprised, I had met him a long time ago. I hardly thought he would have died so early.

"I'm so sorry," I said. And I was, even though I knew they had never gotten along.

"Don't be. I hated him for never taking an interest in me. He always, only, thought about himself. Still, you only get one father, maybe I should have taken an interest in him." An ironic smile appeared on his lips as he rhetorically spoke those last words.

At this point the beers arrived, and we clinked our glasses. A sound to us more powerful than any words.

"Prosit!" Martin said, looking at my eyes.

"Prosit," I replied, my gaze lost in the midst of the beer.

Prosit is the Latin way of saying cheers, literally it means profit. Every time I heard that word, it brought me back to my youth.

"If you don't mind my asking, who was that kid, the only one crying?" I said, trying to change the subject.

"That would be my stepbrother. My father eventually remarried after my mother left him. I never really got to know him, my brother, well my father as well, I guess." He took a sip from his beer, and just looked at it for a while.

"That was a mistake," he said, with the faintest note of shame.

"I'm going to take care of him now though, financially and whatnot."

"Didn't your father leave him any inheritance?" I asked.

"His fortune has been gone for a long time now. Wasted," he said shaking his head.

"You know, I always thought you two were very similar people, you and your father. Why you never got along was a mystery to me."

"He used to be a very lovable person. When I was a kid we used to spend, some, time together. Somehow though, over the years boredom overtook him. I suppose he got sick of me. Or, perhaps we got sick of each other. I don't know…"

I listened to his words intently. He looked down for a while, then looked at me.

"You know I finally realize it, you might be right," he said. I remained silent, waiting for a follow up.

"The conversation we had this morning, about accomplishment and Legacy. Part of the reason why I disliked my father, was because in him, I saw, an older, unchanged version of myself. And now; here I am, pushing forty and exactly the same as when I was nineteen."

A few minutes passed, allowing those words to sink in. "We're the lost generation," I whispered, staring directly into the cataphraction. Incidentally I had referred to one of Martin's favorite authors. But this time there had been no war to keep us from flight, outside of the war we had fought, and lost, within our very souls. He had been in the process of raising his glass, when he put it back down on the table, looked at me, and nodded gravely.

Chapter 2

As I Was...

Everyone in my world wants only one thing: money. The people who don't have it, will end their lives towards it, and the people who do have it, will die to protect it. But where is the honesty in a society where everyone is driven by the same fear of poverty, including me?

I must find it, and *face my fear*.

"But I have lived, and have not lived in vain:
My mind may lose its force, my blood its fire,
And my frame perish even in conquering pain;

But there is that within me which shall tire Torture and Time, and breathe when I expire."

I read the inscription on the statue of Lord Byron, as the rain poured down profusely from the sky, the infinity of which was frightening. Soaking wet, I stood there, ignoring the weather and the cold. And the confidence in the words of a romantic poet, compensated my own lack of strength.

It was a school day, but no school in the world could interest me. So I preferred walking in the park of my childhood, reminiscing and trying to find a way to get around my fear of life. I needed to be alone. Even for only a few minutes a day. I needed a time when I could take off the masque of the young millionaire, or the good student, and be myself. But it never helped. I went on the day after doing the same things as always, and feeling no better than the day before. I had managed to conceal the boredom and the uncertainty, using yet another façade. The people around me, admired and trusted me. I was the only one who knew of the emptiness and weakness that lay deep down, and forced me to adopt my many poses. The poses and roles that my reality had always inclined me towards. But deep down, I knew I would never accept any of those poses, and eventually, I would find myself.

When the rain stopped, the sun came out from behind the clouds. I walked back home on the road I had taken a hundred times. The morning was over, I would step out of the good student and become the young millionaire. At school, in the mornings, I kept my distance from classmates and teachers. They appeared so boring to me, and the thing which bothered me most about them, was that my life was no more interesting than theirs. If you took away all the money I had, and the illegitimate sense of entitlement, I was just as clueless and foolish as them. Of course I could have gone to a different school, someplace where all the students were as rich as I was, and the teachers wouldn't test us, in fact it would be the other way around. That's what all my friends had done, the ones from outside of school, with whom I drank as a gentleman and spent money as a degenerate. But I could not live my entire life on some privileged island of wealth and corruption of the mind. As long as I maintained different identities, I could survive, being no one. But I didn't want to *survive* and I didn't want to fall into a category or label of any sort. What I really wanted was to live, with the courage to be outstanding, regardless of my surroundings.

Back in those days, before our discovery of the Jerry Thomas, we spent our time in a nice place known as "the Felix". It was lost in the back streets near the pantheon. Considered a myth by some, and a lively circle by others, who spent their days there, unsure if by choice or force. The entrance was under stated, almost *hidden*. It looked like any other old, and neglected, apartment building door. Most of the time you had to ring to be let in. Sometimes, on request of the more trusted clients, we would have a password established. The atmosphere inside was more that of a masonic country club than a public café.

That afternoon I walked in, stepping into the door was like stepping just a little further into the void of anonymity, which I promptly ignored. Back then the novelty of things, gave the cunning illusion of excitement. The concept of responsibility, and legacy, still loomed in the darkness behind the light.

Walking in, the first person I saw was Jack. He must have been coming from the bar, which was just beyond the entrance. I had known him for a long time and he was a part of my most intimate circle of acquaintances. He was a reasonably pleasant person to be around, provided he was kept in a good mood by the ones around him. His main problem, other than the standard ones we all shared, was that he was a terrible drunk. When he drank he always got angry, sometimes even with his friends. In that particular way he truly was nothing like the rest of us. Drinking tended to make us more innocent and appear ingenuous. At the time it was just another way to joke about our recreational alcoholic frenzy, now I see it as what it was. It was nothing other than the puerile reflection of a desperate self-righteous attempt to masque our true nature, the weaker side of our personality. Anyways, returning to Jack, luckily for us he was so big that it took a while for him to get tight. He was about 6' 4", though from a distance you couldn't tell, really. Some people are tall and skinny, not him, he was one big Jewish–. He boxed, among other sports. His overall appearance was as intimidating as should be. He had dark skin, edgy features and he always kept his hair short, sort of like a military cut.

We called him Jude, it's German for Jewish. Not that we had any racial prejudice or something of the sort, we just did it to piss him off, pushing him to the edge of his etiquette.

"Hey, Max!!" Jude said.

"My favorite kosher little friend!"

He must have been in a good mood because he took it surprisingly well.

"Come in," he said, smiling.

The main hall, just beyond the entrance, had a wooden bar, adjacent to the wall on the right. The rest of the room was occupied by spacious couches, filled with people centered around antique coffee tables. The walls and the ceiling were adorned with beautiful frescos of epic scenes from a great classical culture. We walked to the far side of the hall and opened a door on the right-hand side wall. Escaping the general racket, we entered a room the manager generously conceded us, in return for our faithful clientele and other favors, of course. It was about half the size of the main hall. Two of the four walls were occupied by wooden libraries maybe 20 feet tall. The other two had paintings on them, mainly 17th century. The baroque era, what a wonderful time. The cultural movement which was afterwards called "Barocco" was born in Rome at the beginning of the 17th century. It was a period of transition between the religious fanaticism which dominated the Middle Ages and, to some extent, even the renaissance, and the age of enlightenment which took place in the 18th century and inspired the French, and the American, revolutions. The foundations of reason and modern times. If only that light shone as far as I had drifted away, I thought to myself.

But, as for history, the *massive* individualism, the destructive nihilism, and its mendacious consequences on society, were still to come. And eventually they would die in hope, in the hope which would inevitably arise when people accept the fall from the idols, as a lack of flight of the human race.

The books in the libraries varied, mostly among classical literature and philosophy. The only two interests which in some way dignified that way of life, *the beginnings*. The rest of the room was occupied by two leather couches. There was a big fireplace on the wall opposite the entrance. Giorgio Altemps was sitting in the middle of one of the couches, occupying a big portion of it. He was a little overweight, and he didn't care. Claudia, his girlfriend, was sitting on his lap. I didn't like her, and she liked him for his money. We all knew it, probably even Giorgio, though of course we were all far too polite to confront him. That was his father's job, when the day came.

At this point they all got up. I shook Giorgio's hand and gave Claudia a kiss on the cheek.

Joey had been sitting on the couch in front of Giorgio. He was short, dark and hairy. He had short hair, a five o' clock shadow at two-thirty and a benevolent smile always pasted on his face. He wasn't particularly bright, but he did have a great sense of humour, you couldn't catch him on a bad day. We called him ape. A fitting nickname, I always thought. I said hello to him and was immediately put in a good mood by his naïve attitude.

The other two people in the room I didn't quite recognize, but I was sure I had seen them before. I definitely had seen her before; she wasn't easily forgotten. Aesthetically, she was utterly flawless, simply beautiful. She embodied the best of classical and modern beauty, as her sumptuous curves met her sharp features and fit body. She had shoulder-length blonde hair, high cheekbones and big puppy eyes. She wasn't cute, or handsome, yet rather ravishing. Her beauty was effortlessly aggressive. She gave the impression of a dangerous person, the kind that never fails to mesmerize even the most confident. And crush your pride.

I don't remember what she was wearing, but it was something unsophisticated and devoid of useless accessories. I forced myself to take my eyes off her and maintain my impeccable manners.

He was reasonably handsome. He had dark hair, fair skin and an interesting face. His expression had a great nostalgic quality about it.

He, the stranger, spoke in an emphatic way, like either he was an expert on every subject or that's just how convicted he was.

"Max, meet two good friends of mine," Giorgio said.

I walked towards her, feeling uneasy.

"This is Ashley," he said.

She smiled at me. I extended my hand and she took it gracefully

"And this is–"he was cut off.

"Martin, pleased to meet you," the stranger said. His words were not eager or emotional. He sounded sure of himself in a non-arrogant way. I figured he and Ashley were together. It was revealed to me later by the ape, who no doubt had had the same thoughts as I. We had a couple of drinks and discussed politics while the girls and Joey, just sat there ignoring us. Of course Claudia was quick to flirt and suck up in any way possible to her prey. Ashley, who was sitting opposite to Martin, just looked at him with dreamy eyes. I couldn't help but think she didn't have a mean bone in her body. Contrary to her appearance, she was ravishing and stupid. The two best qualities a girl in our circle could have. As later on I would quickly become, Martin was utterly bored with her.

Somehow, in all these conversations I was used to being cornered. All of my social circle rotated around a privileged interest, therefore it was impossible for them to have an embracing view of any topic. Being a part of their world, I still couldn't bring myself to be, and think, as they did. I believed in people, all people. It was very difficult for me to estrange any human being, especially those different from us. *They* just couldn't understand this. After all, I guess it was only human nature that pushed us to the easy path of climbing to success over the bodies below. Still, it didn't seem very *humane* to me.

"You're not listening to me! I'm saying that economic prosperity for anyone must, *must*, derive from a policy that aides the economy as a whole. Whether you like it or not you are part of a community," I said to Giorgio after a half an hour of bickering and perhaps one too many grappas.

"Well that's just great, as always the wealthy classes are forced to carry the others. I don't understand you. You and I are not enemies, we're from the exact same social class. –Not quite actually, my parents worked for a living, Giorgio's did not–

"We should be on the same side fighting the labor unions," he said, chuckling as he gave Claudia a pat on the ass. I was beginning to get nervous, the word "fight" bothered me. Wasn't he the *hypocrite*? When had he ever entered politics or stood up for his beliefs? We were all *do for nothings*, so why wouldn't he just resign, and embrace his life as it was, rather than fall further into the void. I couldn't reply out of fear of embarrassing the both of us. But I wanted to.

Martin, stepped in.

"You're suffering from the same problem. You're blinded by a bias interest.

"Look, we can throw around words like community and such all we want; but really, would any of us take action and do what we know to be necessary at the cost of a great personal sacrifice?"

I could not do it as well as him. I could not admit how pathetic we were without feeling shame as he did, devoid of remorse or denial, without false hope or the shield of an idol; only honesty. And nostalgia. Nostalgia for the present in waiting of his fall, which had yet to be, but he knew as real.

We all took a long sip in silence.

Jack broke in.

"You're right, we're locked in a catch twenty-two. The only solution is to keep doing what we've always done. If history has taught us anything, it's that in one way or another, people like us always survive," Jude said raising his glass, toasting to his own statement. But no one else took a single sip, or noticed he had spoken. He laughed awkwardly and looked at the ground.

"You know what, the real problem is? The ape started − the real problem is this tastes absolutely horrible," he said pointing to a 20-year-old vintage grappa. Joey stomped his foot and tilted his head in the direction of the waiter, who had been standing near the door awaiting his politest order.

The poor fellow, who had been trained to know the meaning of the primitive gesture, nodded and headed for the bar to fetch the beer, the ape turned towards us and laughed.

"So, anyway, I'm throwing a party at my country house tonight," Giorgio said between sips.

"Black tie?" I asked.

"No, it's a barbecue," he continued, "I'm getting the meat brought down from the ranch in the Fassone." The Fassone is a region in the north of Italy which is grazed by some of the world's finest cows.

We spent the rest of the afternoon drinking and laughing. However hard I tried I couldn't take my eyes off Ashley. Even when I wasn't looking at her, I obsessed. She had this way of always looking happily naïve, the sort of girl that really can make a man dream. And the ape stared at her with an idiotic grin. Once in a while she would smile back at him, as if she were looking at a baby or a retarded child and she felt sorry for him, but at the same time she thought he was cute. He was lovable, the ape I mean. I had known him since kindergarden. When you looked at him, you couldn't help but think it wasn't so long ago.

It finally got to be about time for everyone to go home and change before Giorgio's party. After a fight over who got to pay the bill, I won. The others promised to buy some rounds some other time. I signed the receipt and downed the last of my grappa. The ape chugged half a pint of beer and let out a loud burp. Ashley gave the rest to Martin, who was thrilled to oblige.

We made our way out as we exchanged pleasantries with the owner, while Joe winked at the waitress. As I left I felt the weight of the books on the shelves and the gaze of the paintings collapse on me, like the foundations of a building which had been badly contrived and misused.

We said our goodbyes, Giorgio reminded us of the address to his country house even though we knew perfectly well how to get there, and then we got on our mopeds and motorbikes. It really was the only way to get around Rome. The streets in the center were far too narrow for our oversized sports cars and SUVs. Besides finding a legal parking space was always a nightmare.

Anyway, I went home swerving through the Roman traffic on my moped. Cars honking their horns left and right, people yelling out of their windows and throwing their hands in the air; in hindsight it really was obscenely *dangerous*.

I got home no more than five minutes later. When I got in the door I saw my father sitting on the couch in the living room. He looked like he was getting ready to go out. There he was, all dressed up in a tuxedo, just reading a book on the couch, a cigar in the ashtray. His skin looked fresh and washed, the product of all the face creams and best treatments in the world. His red hair, of which he still had lots, thanks to all the transplants, was coiffed back with style and all the attention given by the best barber in town. My father was in his late sixties and, just like everyone else his age and with his resources, he was desperately fighting against time. He held his pose of the impressive, successful, business man, but I for one had always been very unimpressed.

"Hey," I said.

"Hey," he said without lifting his head.

"How was school today?" he said with an uninterested tone.

"Same as always," I replied. "Are you going out tonight?" I asked.

"Yes, your mother, is still getting ready," he said, bored of the conversation.

"Can I have the Ferrari tonight?" I asked timidly.

"Yes, your mother, doesn't like fast cars anyway. She thinks they're dangerous," he said rolling his eyes. She thought they were dangerous, but she didn't mind her son driving them. At this point my mother came down the marble staircase opposite the glass door to the balcony. As soon as the upstairs door opened, my father threw the cigar out the window and started waving his hands frantically. I shook my head, especially since, knowing my mother, there was no way she ever would have noticed. She was wearing a red dress by Valentino, and various pieces of jewelry which complimented her dyed blonde hair. She threw her hands in the air in excitement, came towards me and gave me a big kiss, staining my cheek with lipstick. She was always making a big fuss over just about anything. We got used to it after a while.

"Dear, have you gotten the car yet?" she inquired in her petulant tone, as she looked at the mirror above the fireplace.

"The garage is 200 meters away; don't you think we could walk?" my father said protesting.

"Walk?!? I'd like to see you walk on the dirty hard sidewalk in these shoes!! Aren't you the selfish one..." My father left, quietly shutting the door to his study behind him. I did the same going upstairs and my mother kept complaining to an empty room as she looked at herself in the mirror.

I quickly changed and threw on a corduroy jacket. The garage was in the basement of the building next to ours. I walked on the sidewalk, looking forward to driving the car. I got there and waved at the intendant as I made my way towards the Ferrari.

"Max," a voice said behind me. It was Philip Randen, my godfather and my father's attorney. A man of about forty, cultured, successful and rich. I had always respected him because, as most lawyers are, he was a reference point to me, a small window of reason on the madness. He was wearing a black suit which fit perfectly on his composed posture.

"It's good to see you," he said, taking off his right glove and shaking my hand.

"Good to see you too. How are you?"

"I'm alright, thank you. I'm here to pick up your parents. What about you? Still living the life of the young millionaire?" A touch condescending but bearable.

"Something like that."

"Yes, I see…" he said, looking at the Ferrari.

"I worry about you, Max."

"How come?" I gave him a puzzled expression and he didn't say anything for a while.

"Well, I know it's not my place…" He chuckled.

"No.

"I appreciate it," I said. He nodded at me in recognition and I got in the car.

"Try and get rid of those bags under your eyes."

"Will do!" I said as I took off in the magnificent machine.

The drive up was about a half an hour long. The place was just outside Rome, in the beautiful surroundings of the wine growing region of Frascati. The villa was situated on top of a hill. You could see miles in the distance, from up there. Around the hill was all the land attached to the estate, used for growing olives and grapes, to make oil and wine. The eight-cylinder engine of the powerful Italian sports car roared as I pushed it to the edge, swerving around every corner with dead accurate precision and a touch of anger in my veins.

When I got to the estate the gate was open, I drove in and caught up with Jack. He had stopped his Aston-Martin and was speaking to someone I didn't know. I violently revved up the engine of the California to let him know I was behind him and I wanted to get moving. He gallantly stuck his middle finger out the window and started down the driveway. As we parked our cars Martin pulled in next to me, splashing the gravel under his tires. He was driving a jaguar e-type, the one from the sixties with the long hood. He got out of the car and gently closed the door. The expression on his face was unequivocal: *emotional turmoil*. His state surprised me. Even though I had only known him for half a day, in that moment, I could have sworn he was the most confident of all. In an Elysium of noble and civil titles, if anyone was truly entitled in some way, it could only have been the person I barely knew.

"Something the matter?" Jack said.

"Ashley and I broke up."

I should have restrained myself, and focused on more important issues than lack of companionship. I failed in my attempt to resist our human propensity to lust.

"I'm sorry to hear that," I said.

"Don't be, I broke up with her."

"She's moving to Prague next year. She wanted to maintain a long-distance relationship. I think that stuff doesn't work, at least for me."

"Move to Prague," Jack said.

"I'm staying," he stated.

"How'd she take it?" I asked.

"Not so well, she's considering it a lack of interest towards her on my part or something like that," he said thoughtfully.

"Don't beat yourself up, man," Jude said patting him on the shoulder.

"I hate to do this to her, she doesn't deserve it. But right now I honestly don't give a damn."

"Trust me, she'll get over it. They always do" I said, in a surprisingly uplifting tone.

"Yeah, it's always like they're gonna kill themselves for the first week, and then after that they can't even remember your name," Jack said.

Martin raised an eyebrow at him, but he wasn't looking.

"He's right though you know, a month tops and this whole thing'll be gone."

"Let's go inside, you must be hungry," Martin said, getting off topic.

"Me too," the ape had just pulled up in his Ford Gran Torino.

We walked out of the parking lot and headed down the road that lead to the double staircase entrance. The villa had been built in the early 19th century by one of Giorgio's ancestors. The main building was at least a hundred feet tall. The white columns at the entrance recalled a classical style, which persisted throughout the structure. Once you were up the double staircase that led down to the driveway, you would enter a tall wooden door, leaving the gorgeous view of the roman countryside behind you.

We walked side by side, Martin a half a step ahead of the rest. The long hallway that led from the entrance to the internal courtyard, was decorated with portraits of Giorgio's ancestors.

"Hey, wait a minute, that guy in the painting looks familiar" Joe said.

"They're ancestors of the Altemps family" Martin said.

"Oh, I get it" the ape said looking confused.

"What does ancestor mean" he whispered to me.

"Never mind I'll tell you later".

As we made our way into the courtyard, Giorgio excused himself from his party and came to great us.

"Hey, glad you could come. Well, you know everyone here, bar's over there, meat over there -He said pointing in different directions- and the beer, is in the kitchen -He winked at the ape, who laughed and gave him a thumbs up-."

The courtyard had a large fountain in the middle with a water pump held by the statue of a mermaid. On the sides adjacent to the main building were two smaller ones with secluded walkways, behind a row of short and slender marble columns entwined in layers of rampant jasminoides. The side opposite the main building ended with a travertino balustrade beyond which was a magnificent view and a frightful cliff.

Martin excused himself and went towards the edge of the courtyard and looked at the view. Giorgio went back to the front door as a good host. The ape, Jack and I, stood in the middle of the courtyard filled with people.

"It's pretty crazy uh," Jack said.

"What?" I said.

"Martin and Ashley breaking up. How the hell do you break up with a girl like that?" Jude said. Gossip was not appropriate, but Jack had his own way of retaining his etiquette.

"They broke up?" the ape asked with enthusiasm.

"Yes," I said.

"Great, were is she?" he said as if he were a child waiting for his birthday present.

"She's not here yet, but I wouldn't do anything stupid if I were you. She's probably very vulnerable, you'd be taking advantage," Jack said. The ape was puzzled.

"Yeah, besides Martin is right here, it wouldn't be fair to him. Plus, you'll make a fool of yourself, I guarantee it" I said.

"Well, that's going to happen regardless"

"Hey, man! What's up?" said a voice behind my shoulders.

"John! How are you?" I said.

John and I had met because our fathers *did business* together. I had never really liked him much. He was a bit annoying and he thought a lot of himself, as he looked down on other people through his waspy glasses. He had the bad habit of interrupting conversations.

"Not bad," John said.

"I didn't know you came to these things," I said.

"I usually don't. But I could spare the time tonight and, man, leave it to Giorgio to get good food." He laughed and pointed at his stomach.

"You know what I'm saying..."

I let out a forced chuckle and Jude and the ape were silent since they hadn't yet been introduced.

"So what about you. Long time no see," he said.

"I'm alright, you know, just surviving..." I said grinning.

"By the way this is Jack – they shook hands – and Joey – John extended his palm and the ape slapped it–.

We were used to the awkward situations Joey got us into.

"So, anyway, we were just talking about a little situation that has developed here: a friend of ours has just broken up with his girlfriend and Joey wants to make a pass at her. You always were a man of good judgment. What do you think?"

"Is this friend of yours here?"

"Yes," I said.

"Then you simply can't," he said looking at Joey, "it's bad manners."

"Screw manners, and what's this crap about the advantage, I have the advantage because–" he paused and looked at us, as if trying to remember what to say, "she's vulnerable."

Trying to correct him would have been useless, I shook my head as John frowned at him, unsure of where this creature who drove an American car and drank beer from a bottle had come from.

"Where'd Giorgio say the beer was?" he asked us.

"In the kitchen Joe," I said and he went back towards the mansion.

John looked at me.

"Don't take him the wrong way, trust me he's a great guy. Just a little…"

"–Primitive," Jack cut in.

"Ah, I see. Yes, as a matter of fact I heard he has a remarkable tribal tattoo on his right arm to identify himself."

We set our eyes on the bar.

"What are you drinking?" Jack said, his hand on my shoulder.

"Americano," I proposed.

"Let's go."

"You coming, John?" Jack said.

"No thanks, I'm good," he said waving his hands. Poor guy, he always did have trouble holding his liqueur.

"Alright I'll catch up with you later, man," I said.

"Yes. Good to see you."

I nodded and headed for the bar.

We ordered our drinks and talked about how beautiful the villa was as the bartender made the Americanos. We were in cahoots on the fact that the villa was something of an emblem, of what we all aspired to. That cornucopia of art, class, and wealth, was the single greatest thing we could want, our maximal aspiration. It was no secret we were all jealous of our friend and the Altemps family.

The Americano is a cocktail made of Campari and red vermouth, its taste is sweet yet with a powerfully bitter aftertaste. As we finished our drinks, Ashley came out of the hallway and walked down the stairs to the courtyard. She was wearing a white dress cut a little above the knees. She had a gold necklace and gold earrings. Her high heels boosted her already perfect height to about 5'10". Giorgio quickly went to greet her.

"Come on, let's get something to eat," Jack said nudging me and waking me from my trance.

We put two empty glasses on the tray of a random waiter for the last time, and headed for the perfectly disposed tables. Everything was tastefully positioned in the Italian garden. As we sat down for dinner, I was momentarily shocked by how similar we all were. One of the final paroxysms in my faith crisis, which had been developing for the longest time. In our country-casual attire, we all looked like a bunch of puppets, putting on some show of lavishness and tastelessness. Quickly, I convicted myself to the belief that I was the only spectator, and everyone else were the puppets. I exhaled in relief, and slowly eased into my chair.

The meat was great, the taste was strong and needless of condiment. Really good meat only needs oil and salt.

The organization and disposition was impeccable, there were about forty people, sitting at four different tables. Giorgio sat with us. We drank the excellent wine from his cellar and he bragged about all the great ratings he had gotten. All the intellectuals and sommeliers who had praised it, were of course present. I found it interesting, but my knowledge on the subject wasn't strong enough to give an important contribution to the discussion. Martin, on the other hand, gave an art critic who was sitting at our table a run for his money, making connections here and there and showing off his great general culture. Always in his own way, authoritarian but not sanctimonious.

Nevertheless, this person I had just met, Martin, made me feel uncomfortable. While he was unescapably authentic, he was exposing me for what I was, a fraud, a stand in who didn't actually belong. And that was the reason why I envied him.

Ashley, sat at another table far away from us with her friends. The ape made an effort to pass from beer to wine, God only knows if he could tell the difference. When he'd gotten drunk enough he went over to her table a few times and struck out. Each time though, she let him off easy.

Once in a while we exchanged glances and I looked away, timidly. I could not get her out of my mind, and believe me, I was making an effort.

Around sundown, when there wasn't a drop in the last bottle of wine, people started excusing themselves and going home. It had been a wonderful evening and everybody had expressed their gratitude to Giorgio. When all of the guests had gone, Giorgio invited us inside for a nightcap. He turned towards Martin to say there was a particular grappa we must try. I told him I'd be a second. I went to the side of the courtyard opposite the main building and rested my hands on the balustrade as I looked at the valley and its vineyards. I enjoyed the view and smoked a cigarette as the sun was setting, especially late, even for the summer clock. I sipped my half empty glass of wine as the last rays of light shone on the crops and I was already half drunk. I picked up one of the empty bottles from a table and read a small quote from the back of the label which stuck in my mind.

"Where the generosity of nature, meets the humbleness and hard work of man, a great wine is born."

As I daydreamed, lost in deep thought, I was interrupted by a southing female voice.

"Hey." The golden rays of sunlight reflected on her fairly tanned skin, her expensive jewelry, her dark eyes and her blonde hair, which blew lightly in the wind. Her young skin was smooth and soft, and decorated by a sensual tattoo near the small of her back.

"Hey," I said, looking at her with as much cool as I could muster. She was shivering so I automatically gave her my jacket. She smiled and put it on.

"Great view, isn't it?" I continued.

She looked at the horizon, and then turned back towards me.

"I didn't come out here for the view," she said. Her eyes saw right through me. Through all of the good manners and social etiquette, through the façade and the mask. Through my pride.

I was torn, here she was, the object of my desire, yet I had to restrain myself to a set of beliefs. To behave like a gentleman when all that really mattered was to live like a human being, with passion, and love. My heart raced as I desperately tried to make a decision. The decision to be strong.

"God help me," I murmured. I drank the last of the wine, turned my eyes towards her and said,

"Let me escort you inside." My tone was cold and mature.

She looked at me, perhaps embarrassed, or maybe simply surprised. She had managed to seduce everyone, even Martin.

It would have been wrong, I thought. But it wasn't wrong because it was improper, it was just wrong.

"Thank you," she said, apparently sincere.

"For what?"

"For being so polite." She smiled at me, and quickly recovered.

We made our way into the living room of the mansion. Martin, Giorgio, the ape and Jack were inside chatting light-heartedly.

"I should get going," Ashley said.

"I'll give you a ride," Jack volunteered. That was convenient, I thought, since Giorgio was sleeping over and I would not have felt at ease.

We drank some grappa while we talked about the past and the present. It was indeed very good, the slightly darker than usual liquid gave a warm, even feeling as it went down your throat and gracefully burned your insides. Once we had all gotten our fill, which is to say enough to digest our meal, but not to *compromise* our driving, we thanked Giorgio for a lovely evening. He said it was a pleasure and that we were all very welcome anytime. We all exited the living room and made our way to the front door. At this point we said goodbye one last time, walked down the stairs and started for the parking lot.

Martin and I cautioned Joe to drive safely, he laughed and sent us to hell, speeding off in the powerful Gran Torino.

Martin was about halfway into his car when he emerged slightly.

"Oh, Max."

I turned around.

"I appreciate it," he said.

"What?"

"You know." He winked, got into his car, and pulled out.

Chapter 3

Madness and Cataphraction

I woke up the following morning and had breakfast while I smoked and watched the sunrise from my terrace. Looking at the twilight rise into the day, seeping through the arches of the Coliseum and lighting up the old town, I puffed smoke into my lungs, and breathed in the clean air of the morning frost. The peace and quiet gave harmony to my disordered life, and allowed me to think clearly, taking vantage of one of the only moments of the day which wasn't blurred by the influence of alcohol.

As I had woken up that morning and enjoyed a tasty hangover and an uneventful day, I continued doing so. Time just *flew by*. Everything was irrelevant and it was seen through the filter of youth. There weren't any holidays, week days, good days, bad days or important days. There was only the echo of laughter, the aftertaste of wine and grappa, and the terrible fear of growing old that we each kept secretly locked up in the closet.

There was nothing to look forward to. All I had were a bunch of fading memories, from a life well on its way to devastation.

I gave up on school as I saw no point in it and I spent my time there just counting the seconds. Once in a while a teacher would interact with me, they would ask why I didn't make an effort, and they would lecture me on how I wasn't living up to my potential. I would nonchalantly defer. This irritated them and once that happened, the situation would deteriorate before my eyes. Before I knew it no one was taking an interest in me anymore, my teachers had given up all hope and my classmates, who had once looked up to me, now saw me as an outcast and someone who had "problems" and didn't quite fit in.

The good sense that would steer a normal person back on course and away from the madness, I had not yet acquired.

I convinced myself that this world of teachers, and people with whom I could no longer connect, was just a condescending conspiracy. Truth is I lacked courage, the courage to face my reality and put an end to my frivolous problems, the courage to help my friends, who were in the same situation as I, and finally, the courage to confront my parents; and demand the guidance and advice I deserved from them, not to mention love.

So as time went on and my life stayed still, I would just wait for that goddamn bell to ring at 2 pm, the end of the school day, so I could go get drunk with my friends. With every day that passed we started drinking more and more, and our topics of conversation slowly degenerated and headed towards being pure silliness and empty chit chat. As a result of this progressive alteration, maintaining the adequate behavior in relation to our *social status* became more complicated.

One afternoon, we were drinking at the Felix. That day we had decided not to go for our private room as usual, but drink in the main hall instead, where all the middle-aged men had their drinks with friends and business partners, or took their favorite hookers. As usual we were being loud and creating the illusion of happiness. A tall, average-looking man, whom I recognized as the manager, slowly and rigidly came to our table. As a dead body emerges from its tomb, his face was pale, his eyes quickly moved from us to his shoes in embarrassment and fear. The hair slicked across his bald head stuck to the sweat on it, and shined as it reflected the light. His hands were a mix of dark red and stone white, as he clasped them together, over and over again.

The scene remained unnoticed as we subconsciously ignored him. After a few seconds Martin got up and quickly walked towards the man, ever so slightly rocking his shoulders. He put his hand on the man's arm with confidence and asked him what the matter was. The man spoke in an inaudible tone such that Martin had to tilt his head and aim his right ear at his mouth, as he nodded, as always, understandingly. But in that moment I got the feeling he understood no more than I or anyone else, and together we formed some sort of perversely clueless crowd. When the manager had finished, Martin walked him a few steps away from the rest of us and spoke to him. We looked at each other, wondering what was going on, and Joe continued catching up on a conversation that had ended a few minutes before.

In the end, the manager smiled weakly, nodded in submission, and went back towards the door that led to his office, walking with considerably more ease. Martin stood for a while, locked in the position the manager had left him in. Then he looked around the room, saw the frescos, and walked towards us. Something was wrong and I had an idea of what it was.

"Perhaps we should talk," Martin said as he sat back down in his chair.

"What about?" someone said.

Martin still had on the same face he had worn while he spoke to the manager.

"Can you tell us or should we start guessing?" Giorgio asked coolly. The irony was missed.

"Some clients have been complaining about our behaviour," Martin said in an apprehensive tone. The moment I heard those words, something stopped working inside me. It stopped adding up, the balance between my confidence and my dissatisfaction, was now an unresolved equation. A hoax, sustained by good manners, my culture, and everything else that gave me a feeling of entitlement. Along with the binding medicine we all consumed.

But I couldn't make any sense of it, there was only confusion, and the inescapable sensation that something had gone terribly wrong in my life. My manners were all I had.

"What?" yelled the ape.

We told him to be quiet and apologized to the people at the other tables, who by now were making no attempt to hide the scorn on their faces.

"Seriously though, we don't need to take this, especially from them," Jude said slurring his speech and pointing away from our table. Giorgio looked at him, disdainfully, and lowered his finger.

"Shut up, Jack," I said, making an effort not to raise my voice, but warily provoking him nonetheless.

"I'll say whatever I want to say! Do not lecture me, Max," he said and downed a half full glass of whiskey. I was pretty resolved on not responding to him. Then he muttered an insult, still loud enough so I could hear it, and I lost control.

"If you maintained a single shred of the etiquette your title commands, I wouldn't have to." I had done it on purpose. I wanted to piss him off. Nonetheless, the moment I said it, I regretted it immediately. Jack's eyes turned dark red, his veins were throbbing as if they were about to pop out of his skin, trickles of sweat ran down his forehead. He looked at me with all the hate I had seen him give his opponents in the ring before crushing them. I never thought he would have given that look to me, of all people.

Martin got up and broke the line of sight between us. "Let's get out of here, we can go over to my place and have dinner, be as loud as we want. What do you say?"

"I'll second that if we can combine dinner with a few bottles of wine," Giorgio said chuckling.

"A few bottles? Let's make it a few cases!" said the ape.

The very idea of eating and drinking and coming home late to pass out on my bed made me sick to my stomach. It seemed so convenient to ignore the unpleasantness. But I couldn't, not anymore anyways. I felt my blood stir in anger with myself that I was prepared to blame on Jack, provoking and stimulating any excuse to pick a fight and add something new and unusual to the evening. I knew this, I knew it all too well, yet I couldn't deal with it, so I gave in, to my emotions and my hate. And my passionate person had the best of me, eventually.

I got out of my chair and pushed my hair back with the palm of my hand.

"I need to get out of here," I said looking at Jack, who by now had calmed down and was staring at me with a smug expression.

"I'll see you around, buddy," I said to him, raising my eyebrows.

I gave him my shoulders, and headed for the exit, without saying goodbye to anyone else. My head felt as if marinated in booze, my body was moving in a trance, and all I could feel was a desperate need for fresh air and a cigarette so I could relax and return my blood pressure back to normal. I was maybe halfway to the exit.

"Hey, take it easy, friend!!" Jude shouted. I kept my cool and surprisingly had the presence of mind to actually think of apologizing to the other customers in the room.

"Will do," I said softly. There was a moment of silence, then I moved quickly towards the exit, starting to regret what I had started. Even though I had not done much in the past half hour, it was the gravity of everything I had done in my life that was suddenly closing in on me as I took a single step towards the exit. Then something happened which should not have happened, but it changed everything.

I could hear Martin and Giorgio whispering to Jack and the Ape laughing in his own way.

"You left your drink. Lightweight." The shout was louder than the ones before and the tone more menacing, the concept beneath the insult particularly disturbing. Only a split second later I felt the hard glass hit the back of my head with a violence strong enough to make me cringe, had my senses not been dulled by having been drunk all day. The cold liquid made its way under my shirt, and descended down my spine, chilling my nerves.

All you need to do is walk out the front door and tomorrow no one will remember this ever happened, I kept thinking to myself.

Just walk out.

I closed my eyes, my blood cooled down, and the anger disappeared. I took a deep breath and shook my head, aware of what was going to happen next.

I quickly spun around, it must have been at least five full seconds after the impact. My pace was self-assured and confident, my head calm and my actions focused. As I approached, I saw Martin holding his hand up in a last attempt to avoid what would happen next, however, he was not standing in my way.

When I was about a couple of feet away from Jack I took a swing and hit him on the jaw with my right fist. He quickly recovered and hit me with his right on my left kidney. The blow had been delivered with power and accuracy. As I bent over in a desperate attempt to regain my breath and had my hands on my knees, Jude charged his deadly left punch and aimed down at my face. He hit about an inch below my eyebrow, around my cheekbone. I fell to the ground under the immense power of the blow. The entire right side of my face felt as if it had fallen off, and there was just a giant hole in its place. He had always been a southpaw. A cut had opened and the blood drip dropped onto the Persian carpet. I struggled to get back to my feet, slowly managing to push myself up. I had lifted my face about a foot from the ground when I caught a glimpse of Joe's face. The warm, harmless smile that was always there, was now gone, replaced by a horrific look of terror. Not unlike the one you might see on an abused child, psychologically or otherwise.

In the background I could hear Martin and Giorgio trying to calm Jack down and take him outside. But he didn't even want to hear about it. The angry drunk wanted to fight, so I got up. After he had nudged me with his foot a couple of times, as he spoke other words which were beneath him and should not be recalled. I got up much calmer than when I had fallen down.

Jude swung at me, but I ducked and missed his punch with ease. I violently slammed my right into his liver, then took a left punch into his right side. He bent over and I crashed my right fist on his chin in an upward strike, throwing him back on his feet. He struggled to keep his balance and favored his right leg. I raised my foot and drove the rigid heel of my shoe on his kneecap. Jude stumbled and supported himself by putting his hand on a nearby table, I gave him one last swing and the mighty Jewish boxer fell to the ground, overturning the table. He was breathing heavily, blood pouring out of his left eyebrow.

I stood in the middle of the room and looked around. Everyone had left, the manager and the waiters were nowhere in sight. Jack squirmed on the floor, struggling to get up. Then he stopped and we crossed glance for a few seconds. I looked at him with indifference, I had not beaten up a friend. I had beaten up a drunk bastard, which is what he was. And so was I.

All of a sudden he stopped trying to get up, fell down to the floor, and started laughing. It was an uncontrolled laugh, his face was red and the veins in his forehead were swollen

"What?!?" I shouted, stretching my arms.

Jack didn't answer though. He kept laughing and spitting drops of blood on the floor.

My eyes fell on the large mirror on the wall in front of me. Blood trickled down my left cheek, continued on my neck, and had pooled in a large stain on the collar of my shirt. I put my finger on the cut, the pain was subdued, but the blood was warm and wet. And it poured profusely out of the open flesh. It was such a perfect cut, precise enough to have been delivered by a razor. It was so flawless it looked fake, but in that instant, like the end of my pride, it seemed considerably real. I looked at the blood on my fingertip and turned my hands over, realizing there was more on my knuckles. I stared into space in awe, as Jack laughed on the ground and everyone else was silent.

The expression on Martin's face, I'll never be able to forget. As Giorgio and Joey were lost in the midst of their cataphraction, staring at an empty bottle of grappa, Martin very slowly raised himself from his seat, buttoned the jacket of his suit, and put his left hand in the pocket of his pants. He composed himself and brushed his hair with the back of his palm. Then he looked down at Jack, who was still caught in his uncontainable laugh. Martin struggled to keep from grimacing, and for an instant I thought he was only one step away from retching in the middle of the room. Resigning from the disturbing vision, he turned towards me. He wasn't angry, the farthest thing from it, and he wasn't disappointed either. I guess he was looking at me in search of something to say or do, to amend the situation. After a while he turned his shoulders on me, and bowed his head. At the time, I thought he was blaming me for something, or ashamed in some other way. But in the wake of it, I must say, he was crushed by his own inability to comprehend the cataphraction of our lives, bequeathing the role to anyone else, capable of the task.

Large drops of sweat came out of my head and wet my face, my eyes were irritated and filled with water, and I was anxious to leave.

In that instant, I realized, no matter how hard I tried to forget and masque the unhappiness in my life, I would never be able to build a man out of myself. Because there is nothing left to build on when it has been destroyed by alcohol. And you yourself, are an alcoholic.

"What have I done?" I said to myself, in a tone low enough so no one else could hear. Jack was still on the ground, he had stopped laughing and his eyes were focused in my general direction.

"I'm sorry, old friend." I spoke those words in anguish, turned around, and left.

Chapter 4

Elope

It doesn't happen very often to a person to feel truly lost, in fact, if chance has it so, it may never happen to you. To feel lost means to realize that everything you used to have, believe, do or even *feel*; no longer has any meaning. It's like being reborn. But to be reborn a part of you must die. And it's not the fear of death itself that holds you from flight. It's the fear of what lies beyond, over the great divide, after the illumination, there is the fear of not finding the will to act, to see things through; and actually do, what your clarity of vision has allowed you to see. Most people have this sort of illumination during the beginning of their lives; but we lack the will to act, and we throw our lives out to see, at mercy of the currents and the tides. Thus becoming another non-existing element of society.

I decided to elope, not out of courage, or any noble value. I wasn't strong enough to deal with my problems. I ran away out of fear. I couldn't stay in the city which had become the emblem of my life, as a member of the remaining noble class, and as an alcoholic, a do for nothing, and a weak human being. What I was really afraid of was not, growing old and having nothing to show for it. I was afraid of living in a plutocratic society where everything was fake and nothing was real. I was afraid of being ignorant, of being affected from an ignorance that doesn't derive from the lack of knowledge, but from the lack of character.

When you are forged into society nowadays, people make you believe that you are special, an individual. They throw around gimmicky and cunning phrases such as "We're all the same" and "We're all different" in a single sentence. Back then I was ignorant, but I did know that *being my own person* was not my natural right, I needed to earn it, I needed to feel thrill and loss as I needed to feel pain and success. And only with that burning desire to find myself, could I be an individual, could I be *strong*. I was hungry and I craved experience, difference, culture, and perhaps even pain. I truly wanted to wake up in the morning and know I had the hardest day of my life ahead, but I wanted to fall asleep in hope, in the hope of making that one day count.

And in the end I would stand on top of the mountain, looking below, indolent and indifferent, for I have fulfilled my destiny. But I felt it as more than destiny, I felt it as duty. I owed it to myself to be able to see through the world, in which we were all participants and no one was responsible. In which the social trends were forged by the dead and the very old, and they strove to determine the destiny of the young and the very strong.

This giant vortex can only be deciphered by being experienced in the matter of life.

Only when you have been reborn, can you raise yourself in a way that is honest, true and pure.

There was nothing left for me in Rome, no friends, no parents, nothing. Not a single person I could go to, just to talk. To feel I could trust someone, and be trusted. The magnificent beauty of the city was the only thing that had kept me going up until then and it was the only thing I was sad to leave.

The emotions I felt that night were the most powerful I had ever felt in my life. My fear quickly transformed itself in the excitement of going away, no luggage, no plans, nothing to look back on, only to look ahead.

I walked around the city one last time, down Via del Corso all the way to Piazza del Popolo. I climbed the stairs up to the Belvedere and gazed down at my city. I walked through Villa Borghese, breathing in the clean air, scented by the recent rain. I walked up Viale George Washington and passed by the monumental statue of Goethe. Also, at the top, I stopped in front of the statue of Lord Byron one last time, and read the inscription, before leaving the park and going down Via Veneto, Byron at my shoulders.

The street where the *dolce vita* had once been the most recent emblem of the eternal city, would soon perish completely. And the entire generation, which had been mesmerized in its magic, was now dying. The hotels were half empty and there was no one left in the cafes. I kept walking for hours, just thinking of where I would go and what I would end up doing with this chaotic life of mine. I stopped by the bank and withdrew one-thousand euros in cash and headed for Termini train station. My instincts told me to take a taxi, but I stopped myself in time, remembering my commitment to a budget. I got to the station and looked at the departures board. The farthest international destination was a night train to Prague, leaving at seven pm. I didn't think twice, I went to the ticket office and, waited in line. It was around six-thirty in the afternoon and the station was full of people. People meeting, leaving together, going home to their husbands, wives, children, girlfriends, boyfriends, who knows?

"Sir! Sir!"

The fidgety woman behind me gave me a push and pointed at the chubby woman behind the glass window. I walked to the desk and smiled at the clerk. She didn't seem very happy, maybe she was nervous, had problems, maybe she was depressed. Maybe that's why there was a half-eaten snickers bar behind the counter. I asked her for one ticket to Prague, second class. She gave me the ticket and pointed at her watch, signaling I'd better hurry if I wanted to catch the train. I smiled once again, took the ticket, folded my wallet in my pocket, and left the desk.

I walked towards the platform calmly, it didn't feel like running away. It felt more like starting fresh, like I was finally free to live, and an immense weight had been lifted off my shoulders. Then again, I was so naïve, and I had no idea what waited beyond the platform.

The train was a few minutes late, and it took a while for the doors to open. Finally, a half-hearted inspector exited the engine car. His uniform was worn-in by years of use and cheap cleaning. The tissue was faded and the once black color of it was now turning grey. He asked me for my ticket and I gave it to him. He pointed in the general direction of my wagon and I set off. Before getting on the train I had a moment's hesitation. Let me put it this way, I felt as if instead of getting on a train, I was getting onto the Santa Maria and heading towards the unknown.

I looked at the platform and the station behind it one last time, thought of my parents, and got on the train.

We pulled out from the cloud of smoke which surrounded the train. It took a few minutes for the wheels to squeak their way to a move. The train was half-empty. On the opposite side of my wagon there was an old couple, not Italian by the looks of it. Later on I heard them speaking in an Eastern European language. They had backpacks as luggage and each other for company. They were wearing old, baggy jeans and colorful raincoats, which matched the man's intense red hair. They looked happy as they held hands. We crossed glance for a few seconds, I wondered who they were, what their story was and what the odds of me ever seeing them in my life were. They were old enough to be my parents and I wondered what I would be, had I been born on the road, without money; without my title…

They fell asleep about an hour after the train pulled out. I looked at the countryside as it passed by. Remembering that people would come looking for me, I thought of getting rid of everything that could be traced. First the credit cards, which hurt the most, and then my phone. I felt bad about littering on the track. Maybe some farmer or someone, would find them and I would make him happy.

The last light of the day gave me a reflection of my face against the glass of the window.

I looked at it and realized something within me had changed; and I would never, ever, be the same. And I could be strong.

Chapter 5

Prague in the Winter

The train shook violently from side-to-side as it changed tracks. I opened my eyes, and finally gave up on trying to sleep. I wasn't used to sleeping in an upright position, much less without a nightcap. It was the month of October, and it was cold. The temperature had gone down since Rome and the rural countryside of the Czech Republic signaled we were getting close to our *final destination*. I tightened my overcoat and breathed into my hands as I rubbed them together. The train had no heating system, either too old or too mal kept. It was a Czech train. I got up to go to the bathroom. When I got there I was shocked to find out the toilet was nothing but a hole in the pavement of the train, from which you could see the tracks below. Anyways, I didn't mind this too much. I washed my face in the sink, which felt dirty and like it hadn't been cleaned in ages. The cut from the night before was healing well, thanks to the cold, and hopefully wouldn't leave a scar. The train shook again from side-to-side as I left the bathroom and went back to my seat. The old couple had woken up too, and was having a bag of cookies for breakfast. The man asked me if I would oblige but I said no and thanked him anyway for his kindness. We pulled into the central station in Prague, my heart skipped a few beats as the train slowed down to a halt. The inspector hurriedly went through the wagons and rudely asked us if we might vacate the coaches. The old couple got their bags from the overhead luggage compartments, the man helped the woman get her backpack on her shoulders, and they headed for the exit. I was a few steps ahead of them so I opened the door and beckoned towards the platform. They thanked me and got out, I quickly followed. That was the last time I ever saw them.

It was cold. I was wearing dark jeans, a white shirt, a brown lightweight sweater and a dark-grey wool overcoat. I moved quickly towards the station with my hands in my pockets. When I got inside I went to the tourism office and asked the clerk if there were any cheap hotels or places to stay in the city center. He gave me a number of contacts but I couldn't understand a word he was saying, so I asked him if he might write it all down for me. He sighed, got out a piece of paper and a pen, and wrote something down. When he was done I thanked him for his time and left. I instinctively felt my coat pocket for my cigarettes and realized I only had about a pack left. For the first time in my life I had to make do with a budget, and cigarettes were a luxury I would have to spare. Still, my head was dizzy from having slept badly, and I overall felt terrible from not having had breakfast, coffee, a shower... As if these were the most important of my problems. So I decided to have a smoke. I stepped out of the station doors and into the morning mist. The fog seemed like liquid cold penetrating into my lungs and biting my insides. I took a cigarette from my silver case and reached for my gold lighter. As I brought the lighter to the edge of the cigarette, my eyes fell upon an old man, who was walking in front of the station. His clothes were worn-in and tattered, his shoes were split apart at the sole. He was unshaven and had on a wool hat and half finger gloves to protect himself from the Czech winter. He looked at the ground and picked up a dirty cigarette butt, smiling at it. It was a familiar smile; one I could have seen on a number of faces I knew. He put the used cigarette in his mouth, turned towards me, and spoke some words in Czech. I deduced he was asking me for my lighter. Shamefully, I admit, my first thought was that he might steal it. Appalled by the scene and feeling guilty for my prejudiced thoughts, I quickly opened my cigarette case and offered him one of mine. I lit it for him and he gave me a warm smile, which broke through his crooked teeth and rough features. I watched, puzzled, as he slowly walked away, his head bowed as he inspected the ground and the garbage cans.

I took out the piece of paper the man at the information desk had given me, and realized there was only one address written on it. A little disappointed by this, I folded it and put it in my pocket.

I stopped a young woman on the street, and asked her if she could point me in the right direction. She said it wasn't very far, and told me how to get there. I walked through the town towards Zizkov, the area where I was to find the hotel. It was in the district of

Prague 3, which is fairly central and not far from Vaklavske Square.

The town was not very busy, it didn't have that rush hour feeling, which is characteristic of a big city, and ends up driving everyone insane.

Walking in, what I hoped was the right direction, I started seeing even less traffic and fewer people. I walked pass a small playground. The swings and slides were made of metal, which was rusting, as time chipped away.

Not far beyond the playground, I spotted the name of the street. It was uphill, so I started climbing, looking left and right. And searching for the hotel. I stopped at a supermarket to get something to eat, in an attempt to subdue the revolting sensation in my stomach. There was no one inside, only a boy at the counter. He had dark skin and edgy features. He reminded me of someone I couldn't quite place.

I walked up the hill as I ate the chocolate bar I had just purchased, and studied my surroundings. The buildings looked old and full of history, the architecture was very much unlike the typical post-soviet style that you might find in Warsaw, or some parts of Budapest. The city had apparently been well-preserved, and not destroyed by the wars.

I got to the hotel and realized it was more of a youth hostel. The atmosphere inside was surprisingly friendly and warm, the main lobby was a pub and the desk clerk was sitting behind the counter sipping a pint of beer. Weird guy, he was. He had silver-coloured hair and thick nerdy glasses. By the smell of him, he hadn't showered in weeks; or perhaps he bathed in beer. I tried to ask him about any vacancies.

He wasn't very helpful since he seemed pretty involved with the beer he was staring at, in a similar way I had seen many other people stare at alcohol. Fortunately, a young girl came out of a back door behind the counter and asked how she could help. It felt reassuring to meet someone who I could talk to, and seemed eager to help me. She had light- brown and blonde hair, and strong east European features, which complimented her round face and small nose. Her eyes were blue, and looked sincere and innocent. Her clothes were old, but clean and fit in well with the pub atmosphere. She was wearing blue jeans and a pink sweatshirt. I asked her for a single room, if possible. She said no problem and told me the charge was fifteen euros a night or 405 chk. I said that would be fine so she took my passport number. I, stupidly, asked her whether it would be traceable. She gave me a weird look and I immediately regretted having asked the question.

"What do you mean?" she said.

"Are you going to insert it into a computer?" I said in a professional, all business tone.

"Uhm, we just need it in case anything happens, until then it will stay written down in the register, OK?" she said, in her sharp accent, pointing at a blue book on the counter.

"That's fine," I said, giving her my passport. I tried to think of something that might justify the question, but I came up with nothing. Only my own stupidity and lack of experience. Fortunately, in the end, my own insecurity was making me appear serious and less clueless than I was. Anyhow, I hadn't done anything wrong. All I had was the fear of my past, so I decided it was a good idea to maintain a low profile, and temporarily vanish into anonymity.

She wrote some stuff down, I filled in a couple of forms, without reading them, and she handed them to the man with the silver hair, who grunted and took them in the back. She gave me the key to the room and told me it was on the fourth floor. I left the lobby/pub through a heavy metal door, and started up the wooden staircase. The wood was rotting and made an ominous noise every time I took a step. The railing was also particularly precarious, and I didn't dare touch it. I got to my floor and took a while to associate the room number with the door. It was wooden and the lock was weak, which worried me a little. I would have to find a safe place for my cash. God knew, I couldn't afford the risk of carrying it with me. The door opened with a good push and another one of those ominous noises, the ringtone of weakness, somehow I was already accustomed to. The room was cheaply furnished, but spacious and had a window with a good view of the city. I saw there was a small heater, so I fiddled with it until I managed to turn it on. Exhausted, I lay down on the bed for a while, trying to figure out my next step. I had about nine-hundred euros and counting, the room would cost me fifteen euros a night. That meant to support myself further I would need extra funds. Get a job. But where? And what?

I had no skills, no contacts, nothing. Frustrated, I decided to gout for a walk. I wedged half the cash between the wall and the radiator, which soon would be boiling hot and hopefully dissuade any unwelcome guest from prying behind it.

As I got closer to the city center, I started seeing more people on the streets. They seemed quiet and minded their own business. It was very much unlike Rome. In Rome everyone would be on the streets or in the bars drinking coffee, the traffic would be blocked and full of angry taxi drivers honking their horns. And the mopeds... The mopeds would be swerving through the cars and occasionally climbing up on the sidewalk, like monkeys in a jungle. Everyone would be in a hurry to go somewhere, do something, meet someone, and then go back home. Here everything seemed quieter, people led a calm lifestyle, apparently. Maybe it was the cold. In any case, I rather liked the change. It gave me a chance to hear myself think, to think clearly. It was relaxing, which was odd since I had just ran away from home, and desperately needed to come up with a plan, something that might help me get on my feet and make some money. For now, I had enough cash in my pocket to get by.

I got to Vaklavske Square and walked passed all the closed strip clubs and the pubs. I continued all the way to the river and crossed St Charles Bridge. On the bridge there were a few tourists taking some pictures of themselves as they made awkward faces, and posed in front of the gorgeous view of the Vtlava. At this point, I got hungry, so I started looking for a place to stop and have an early lunch. I found a small pub that had a nice terrace on the canal, very close to the Kafka Museum. I sat down and ordered strudel and a Budvar beer, the only real Budweiser. The strudel was wonderful and the beer was fresh and soothed my upset stomach. I suddenly realized, this was the first time I had ever drank alone, it felt good, like I was drinking for the sake of pleasure instead of pressure. I finished eating and downed the last of the beer. After I had settled the bill and taken a business card from the desk, I left the restaurant feeling much better than when I had walked in. The rest of the day was spent walking around the city. Finally, I gave up on trying to think of a way to earn some money, a next step of some sort, and decided to just let time take its course and see what the future would bring. Serendipity.

I went back to my hotel, not defeated or apprehensive, but self-assured and, unconsciously, full of all my dauntless youth.

I had a steak down at the bar while I chatted with the woman who had checked me in. Her name was Angela. We talked about where I was from, what I planned to do in Prague. I sidestepped some of the questions, and gave some vague answers here and there. Maybe I shouldn't have though, perhaps it would have been wiser to make that leap of faith and open up for the first time in my life. She didn't seem to mind my shyness though, and gave me several tips on what to do anyways. For a moment I enjoyed the idea of simply being a lost tourist, but I wasn't. I was a lost human being.

When I finished eating, she put the bill on a tab, I thanked her for the company, and said goodnight. I got up to my room after climbing up the staircase, half drunk, and barely had enough time to take my clothes off before I collapsed onto the bed.

Chapter 6

Moving On

The next few days I felt like a lost boy. I thought of my friends and family, and even of going back home. Then I would look at myself in the mirror, and see something besides the reflection, a reason worth going forwards instead of falling back. I knew my life as I had known it was over. There was nothing left for me. And I was no longer the person I had left behind in Rome.

I had trouble sleeping well, my mind was too stressed to allow me to sleep. It felt good to go running every morning. I guess it was just a way of releasing some tension. It cleaned my lungs from the cigarette smoke, and strengthened my body. Being sober felt good. It felt like being alive, like being free. And I could see what I had been like as a drunk. The life I had led until then disgusted me. It made me angry, angry with myself for not being able to handle my problems and take hold of my life, which had been too good for me since day one. Only after I had already left it all behind, I managed to see what I could have done with it. The power I had, and put to no good use. I was a failure and an indolent. A failure to myself and an indolent to the world I had the power to change.

But the past was the past, and I needed to get on with my life. Start fresh and start over, wiser than before; profiting in some way from my past life and not allowing that memory to become a burden. I owed it to myself to take action and aspire to determination and even strength.

I went to museums and walked around the city. It was very different from Rome and beautiful all the same. I would eat once in a while, when my appetite tickled me, and I would drink in reason, savoring the beer before it went down, and finding pleasure in it that I had never before found in a beverage I had always deemed inferior to wine.

One day, I was walking home after a full day of sightseeing, and felt like having a beer before going to my hotel, as usual. I stopped at a small, out of the way, place in one of the side streets in Zizkov. It was about half-full. People drinking and eating, mostly men, though there were a few women. I sat at the counter and asked for a *pivo*. The bartender grabbed a glass from the counter, and started filling it up from the gold plated tap. He was a big fellow, a little over 6'5", bald at the head, with muscular arms and several tattoos. He had an unequivocal beer gut bulging from under his dirty T-shirt. I sat down at a stool and he handed me the beer, putting it down on the counter with force. The foam spilled over and went down the sides of the glass. I apprehensively swallowed a few sips of the cold Pilsener and felt small, sitting on a stool in a run-down pub from a poor neighbourhood of Prague. The bartender poured himself a shot of Becherovka and drank it, before throwing the glass on the floor. He turned towards me and looked at me, squinting his eyes.

"Give me the money," he said. His tone was low and scratchy.

"Sure," I said, getting out my wallet.

"How much?"

"Give me the money!!" he shouted, yet no one in the bar turned around to see what was happening.

"I will. Here's 100 chk. Alright?" I said, trying to keep cool, but betraying myself in the last word. I was giving him twice the regular price for beer in Prague. He looked at the money and grunted, then put fifty in the cash register and fifty in his pocket. I quietly drank my beer and didn't inquire into the matter, since I didn't want any trouble. I distracted myself by watching the TV, the news was on. All the headlines were in Czech so I couldn't understand anything, but I just looked at the pictures and kept to myself.

"Go!!" the bartender yelled at me. The power of his body odour and his bad breath alone, would have been a good enough reasons to split. But I didn't want to go. I wasn't used to being made out a fool, and something in me found great pleasure in challenging this colossus of a man.

"Why?" I said calmly. He said nothing, caught off-guard by my response.

"I'm sitting down here drinking my beer, why would I want to leave?"

"Not here! Go!"

Someone came up next to me, and politely asked me if he might have my seat, since he always sat in that seat at night. I figured what the hell, so I got up and went to sit down at a table nearby.

I had gotten about halfway through my beer, and the bartender looked at me, seeing or not seeing, I'm not sure. He poured himself a shot of Becherovka and drank it while he chatted with the guy who had taken my seat, and I thought it was the end of the incident. The bartender came over to my table.

"Not here!" he said flexing his muscles.

"Why not?" I said.

"This table, too big."

"Okay, then where would you like me to sit?" I said, mocking him.

"Not here!!!" he yelled at the top of his lungs. I got up and headed for the door, sick of the whole thing.

"You must pay!" the bartender yelled behind me.

"I already paid," I answered without losing my patience.

"No! 500 chk," he shouted.

"I'm not going to give you 500 chk," I said, with all the confidence in the world on my shoulders. Young and dauntless and very, very stupid.

He came towards me – it was obvious now a fight was going to break out. As he moved closer I realized I would probably lose and be lucky to walk out alive.

"Hey, Sven!" shouted someone from the other side of the bar. The man was only a little shorter than the bartender, about as tall as Jack, I thought. He quickly got up and intercepted Sven as he made his way towards me. He punched the bartender, square in the face with his left fist.

"I'm tired of you picking on tourists, you lowlife," he said.

"I do predeye." Roughly translated 'go f--- yourself'. The profanity made me think of how we had always held it in such low esteem, most of us.

Sven punched him in the stomach and the man grimaced in pain, but elegantly avoided a second punch to the face, and retaliated with a roundhouse punch to the jaw. They fought like animals, exchanging brutal punches. I hadn't yet raised a finger, I stood there, doing nothing. Suddenly, Sven grabbed a tall beer glass and was about to crash it onto the man's skull. I was a few feet away, so I leaped towards him as fast as I could. When I was in range I grabbed Sven's wrist and pushed it backwards. Then I slammed my shoulder into him, and he backtracked until he fell, crashing to the ground with a noise loud enough to finally attract the attention of the other distraught customers. The man, who was still recovering from the brutal beating he had taken in my place, stood up straight. When he saw Sven on the ground he didn't think twice and kicked him, two times, violently between his thigh and his calf.

Sven rolled on the ground, touching his thigh and suffocating a desperate cry. His face was red and he had some blood trickling down from his eye. Now men from other tables started getting up and coming towards us. They looked like they were in their forties, long beards and moustaches, dirty clothes and red faces from all the drinking. They spoke amongst each other while looking at us.

"Run," he whispered.

He started running and went out the door, I was only a few strides behind him. The men from the bar ran after us, but they were old and we were young, and fast. We lost them in the neighborhood near the Vtlava, where the streets were narrow and it was easy to break line of sight. We slowed down and I studied my new idol. He looked not much older than me. But there was more experience in his eyes and scars on his face. His features were vaguely defined and they sagged slightly, over the influence of hard times. His body was muscular and powerful, but not in good shape and you could tell the running hadn't been easy for him. He had short brown hair, a hint of wrinkles on his forehead, and a scar on his nose. There was a cut above his left eyebrow and it was bleeding profusely. His jaw was swollen and his pain was evident, even in the cold night.

"Have we lost them?" he asked, panting.

"I think so," I said, regaining my own breath.

"By the way I'm Max. Thanks for saving me," I extended my hand. He looked at it and shook it firmly.

"I'm Mickey. And don't mention it, I probably would have fought him anyways."

"You're a strong fighter," I said with admiration.

"Thanks, you were pretty good too."

There was an awkward moment of silence, or perhaps I was the awkward one.

"What are you doing in Prague?" he asked.

I hesitated, not knowing what to say.

"Come on, I know you're not a tourist. I'm not that stupid," he said, smiling.

"Truth is I don't have a clue. I ran away from home about a week ago and every day I wake up and ask myself what I'm going to do." We didn't look at each other. Nor was it necessary.

"It's the only way to do it," he said staring into space.

"What brings you to Prague?" I asked.

"I'm a drifter," he said, making me feel naïve.

"I came to Europe about four years ago–" he continued, "I work a little here and there and move when I feel like it."

"It's a good life?" I asked with curiosity.

"It's better than what I had back there."

"Speaking of work, you wouldn't know of any job offers or anything like that. I'm kind of running low on cash."

"I'm a construction worker. I bet you could get a job at the site."

"Yeah! Thanks, that would be great," I said, with a sigh of relief. I took out my cigarette case and offered Mickey a smoke.

"Want one?" I offered.

"Thanks." He took a cigarette and put it in his mouth. I took one for myself and handed him the lighter.

"So what's your deal anyway?" he asked, looking at the gold lighter.

"What do you mean?"

"Silver cigarette case, gold lighter, nice clothes. What are you rich?"

"Well, I was, I guess," I said, and the reality of what I had done sunk in deeper still.

"And you decided to leave all that behind. Just give it all up?"

"I had no choice."

"I see…"

"What about you? Do you ever look back?" I asked, quite bluntly. He gave me an odd look, either the question bothered him or he didn't have an answer.

"I'm sorry; I didn't mean to pry."

He took a puff from his cigarette and blew the thin smoke in the cold of the night.

"Sometimes. Sometimes I look back. Wonder what the people I left behind are up to, if they still remember me…" A nostalgic grin appeared on his face.

"Regrets?"

"No. Never."

"Why'd you do it then?"

"I don't know. Because it felt right."

We smoked in silence for a while, and stared into the darkness saying nothing. It was cold and quiet, and we were both young and we trusted each other, even though we had just met. There was something dominant in our lives we both shared, I was sure of it then.

"You know, something you'll find out, someday, is that you cannot run away from something unless you have somewhere else to go. That is what you must focus on." And with that we called it a night and put an end to our laconic conversation.

Mickey gave me an address to show up at the next morning for the job, and a phone number where I could reach him. It was a hard line.

We walked together for a while and then went our separate ways, back home.

It was around one-thirty when I got to the hotel and would have to get up at six the next morning. I took off my clothes, washed up and went to bed. Before closing my eyes, I thought of how much cash I had left, and fell asleep in hope.

Chapter 7

Bittersweet Life

The construction site was on the outskirts of the city. It took me about an hour by public transport to get there, by tram first and then a regional bus. The ride up was long and disagreeable. As I got closer to my destination, and farther from the city centre, people in jacket and tie and Italian loafers got off, and the bus filled with people in dirty overalls and heavy working boots. The expressions on their faces were bored and indifferent, as if they were living life a second time, and had lost all enthusiasm. They had bags under their eyes and wrinkles on their foreheads.

I was beginning to feel a little self-conscious about my appearance, I was wearing the only clothes I had, except the shirt and sweater, with which I would have felt ridiculous. So I had on my jeans and my undershirt, overtop I wore my grey coat.

The driver called out the last stop, and all the men on the bus got off. Not a single woman. Unsure of what to do, I followed the group as they headed towards the large construction site. The works were about halfway through, and the *opera* in question was a typical post USSR style building. The scaffolding had been completed and its large metal pillars rose from the ground about sixty feet high. The cement foundations and floors contributed to the challenging look. It looked like a giant skeleton arising from the ground into the sky.

The weather was the best I had seen so far, the sun was shining on the ground, and it was warm and comfortable. It was not nearly as cold as the misty day on which I had arrived. I stopped at the gate, and hesitated to go in. Fortunately, Mickey came to fetch me. He was wearing a grey T-shirt, stained with white paint, a pair of old jeans, a dark-brown bomber jacket, and a baseball cap. He brought me round to a small mobile office, which had feeble plywood walls and a metal roof. Inside it was minimally decorated with a few plants and some pictures. We went in and Mickey explained to a secretary he had an appointment with "the boss". We waited for about a couple of minutes. There were some chairs, but we were standing. A large man came out of a door behind the secretary's desk. He was not very tall, a little below average. His feet made a thumping noise as he came towards us. Moving his sluggish body, looked like a challenge for him, all three-hundred pounds or so. His skin was tanned and his hands were manicured. His hair was gelled in a somewhat questionable comb over. A thick moustache dominated over his face, which had strong, not so pleasant features, but he kept clean and cared. He was wearing a three-piece, blue pinstriped suit, a blue and white shirt and a red tie with gold dots on it. I didn't like him and I wanted the job.

"What is it?" he barked at us.

"This is a friend of mine; he'd like to work here."

"It would be a pleasure, sir," I said.

He looked at me and my clothes, then frowned down at my Clarks desert boots.

"Sign the papers and get to work," he said.

"Thank you, you've been very helpful." I extended my hand but he did not take it. The awkwardness in the room was like water in a fish tank. And for the first time in my life, I was forced into thinking I was not the shark but merely a goldfish.

The boss left the room and the secretary handed me some papers and a pen.

The only feeling I was left with from that meeting, was the fear of becoming someone I despised. I knew even though I had gotten the job, my journey was far from over.

I glanced at the contract, not the first one I had seen in my life. The workers were unregistered and the safety regulations were lack. I signed and tossed the pen into the secretary's lap. When we stepped out of the office I gasped the fresh air, leaving that fart of a man behind.

"Come on. Lose the coat, man, I'll let you use my locker. Then we'd better get to work or the both of us will get fired," Mickey said.

I put the coat in his locker, which was in another mobile building about twice the size of the first one. As I folded it attentively he broke out in a peremptory laugh.

"I'm sorry, I'm sorry." He wiped the sweat from his face and composed himself. He left his jacket in his locker, which incidentally had no *lock* on it, and we exited the room and headed towards the construction site.

The job was tough and it didn't pay too well, still it was money, and it would hopefully keep me afloat. I would need to get some new clothes, but I could get those for free at a mission church that Mickey knew of. He introduced me to a couple of co-workers. The British was named Hugh, a good man who always kept a wise silence, and a novel at his side. He was in his mid-thirties, dark hair, average build and well-postured. He appeared pensive as he worked, and once in a while he would pause and look at the skyline in the distance. We chatted for a while and he asked me some questions, not particularly interested in the answers. I told him bits and pieces of the story, but nonetheless I got the feeling he somehow already knew the whole thing.

He was very restrained in the way he showed his emotions, very British, or perhaps simply very well-mannered. I was stunned by how such a charismatic person had wound up in such a strange existence. As if he were caught in a limbo between a horrible present and a magnificent past. I asked him some questions, but he answered vaguely and got off topic. Another laconic fellow. The other guy Mickey introduced me to was a Czech, he was from somewhere in the countryside out of town and had come to Prague in search for a job. He was in his late twenties, hairy, had a powerful body and a tribal tattoo on his right arm. His name was Alex, he was engaging and quite sociable. We quickly got along and decided to meet for dinner that night, Mickey knew the place. The rest of the day was exhausting. Since I wasn't a skilled construction worker, my job was to bring sacks of cement and other materials up the scaffolding. It was not the safest job, but I was careful and happy to do the work, so I managed fine. We paused for a half an hour lunch break and went to a nearby pub. We ate a bad sandwich and had a good beer as we chatted light-heartedly. After lunch we got back to work and the rest of the day was uneventful. Later that evening the superintendent told us we had filled our quota for the day and we could go home. We gathered our stuff from the lockers. I put on my coat since it was getting cold and I no longer had the strenuous work to keep warm. We got on the bus and rode back to town. The ride back was silent; I guess we were all too exhausted to talk. Each of us was absorbed in his thoughts, and the cold sweat was freezing on our foreheads. The others got off a couple of stops earlier than I, and we made arrangements to meet that night. None of us had cell phones, so we just gave ourselves an appointment for nine o' clock at the Bell Tower square, everyone knew where it was. I got to the hotel and dragged my aching feet up the staircase to my room. I undressed, had a shower and put on my shirt, which was still relatively clean, but only reminded me I needed to get more clothes. Before starting out I had the slightest thought of staying in, to sleep off the hard day of work, but I quickly dismissed it, finding strength in the thrill of my existence, beyond Rome.

Back then was the first time ever, in which I felt energized, enthused, and most of all full of life. After a while you lose it, as people often do with age, and the presumption of being wise settles in, destroying the youthful struggle and quest for experience. After that, nothing can be done, there's no position, authority or qualification that can justify your hypocritical preaching, because when you speak words from the past which no longer dominate your philosophy, then, they are worthless. Only when you *feel,* instead of reminisce, then what you say is of value, and you yourself are honest and true. And back then I wasn't sure of anything, but I knew that I *felt.*

The city lights illuminated the quaint streets. It was easy enough to find the meeting point. The neighborhood around the square was picturesque and more alive than the rest of the town. There were lots of bars and pubs. It appeared to be a slow night, not many people around, just locals. After all, it was a Tuesday night in the middle of October. When I got there Mickey was already in front of the church and waved his hand as I approached.

"Hey, come on let's go."

"So where are we going anyways?" I asked, a few seconds later.

"It's an out of the way place. Mostly locals."

"Friendly locals?" I asked thinking of the man from the bar named Sven.

He let out a wry chuckle.

"Don't worry, we'll be fine. Just don't steal their beer or anything," he said, seriously.

"Right," I said, unsure of what to make of it.

We got to the place and went in through a small door. Inside it was noisy and warm. The room was filled with cigarette smoke and drunk Czechs with red faces. Old and young people mixed together, socializing eagerly, as if their age had been flattened by the same alcohol they all shared. There were long wooden tables with matching dark wood benches to sit on. The place was more than half-full, so it was evident we would have to share a table with someone else. The atmosphere was very uplifting and cheerful. We sat down next to Hugh and Alex, who were about halfway through their first beer, or perhaps it was the second, or the third...

"You started drinking without us," Mickey said.

"Not a lot; just a little bit," Alex said, mimicking the phrase with his thumb and his index finger. Hugh did the same. Their puerile attitude made me smile and feel instantly at ease.

"Fair enough," Mickey said grinning.

"Let's get something to eat," someone said.

"Yeah, I'm starving, what's good here?" I asked.

"Whatever they have," said Mickey.

"Well, don't we see a menu or something?" I asked.

"No there's no menu," Hugh said.

We got a round of beers, and then several after, and Mickey and I quickly caught up with Hugh and Alex. The beer went down like water and it had an even taste, as a Pilsener should. It was cheap and we all drank various litres each. When you finished a pint one of the waiters would come over, take your glass and raise his thumb, if you raised your thumb back to him then he would bring you another. The food came. It consisted in a meat stew. They brought it in a big pan, the size of a coffee table. We ate with skewers and our hands, not bothering to the cleanliness of the table or our clothes.

A group of old men sat next to us. When they arrived I noticed, notwithstanding their attempts to conceal it, they were already half-drunk. After a few hours they were completely and utterly lost, plastered. Still they kept a decorous attitude, considering the kind of place, and they seemed quite content, as drunkards go. One of them, the one sitting across from me, was very talkative and I spoke to him about lots of different things, while he kept repeating the same phrases. Partly, I guess, because of the language barrier, but mostly, repeating the same things is the key sign of the gracious alcoholic effect. In hindsight I don't know why I used the adjective gracious. The other character from that merry and gregarious group of people was a man who perhaps was a little younger than the others, still probably in his late sixties. All he did during the entire evening was smile at me and attempt to light a cigar, using countless matches. What I remember mostly about him was how much he drank. He did nothing but chug beer and when the waiter would bring him another pint he would loudly say "Danke!" and drink it as he had the earlier one. I would have wanted to count how many beers he had but I lost him as I myself got drunk, and for a second I saw something of myself in that man. Yes it was me! I thought, just older and with a different background. I shivered at the thought and then kept drinking.

In any case, we all got pretty tight, and after that the beer kept coming, and my fear of life faded more and more, with every pint I finished.

Drinking has a tendency to break through your social constrictions, in fact it brings you dangerously close to being free. But not quite there, only close enough so that you can see the ether and fall back down into the void, returning once again to your fear. But the real question is, what are you afraid of? Being free or breaking free of your *habits*? Thankfully back then in Prague, where no one knew me and no one could get to me, I had no habits. I had started fresh and I was at *liberty* to be whoever I wanted.

When we were finished our meal I insisted on paying the bill, to thank them of their friendship, or maybe I was driven by some compulsion to do so, I don't know. Once you've been rich in your life, it's hard to change your approach to money. But I wasn't scared to be who I was. And I was starting, once again, to find a little pride in myself.

Then we said goodbye to the group of old men, and the one with the cigar extended his hand as I was getting up. It was a little awkward, considering I hadn't shaken anyone else's hand; the others, his friends and mine, laughed and giggled, but I took his hand and looked him in the eye.

We walked on the small streets of the neighborhood and wound up at Vaklavske Square, laughing and rocking our shoulders. The night clubs had their neon lights on. As we got closer I realized they were a different kind of club. Alex proposed we celebrate my arrival in town and go to a strip club, apparently a famous custom in the Czech Republic. He innocently stated it was patriotic duty to support the driving industry of the country.

The others quickly agreed in their own blurred judgment, except for Hugh. He protested a little and maintained his position, but in the end he caved in, and followed the group. We went to a strip joint called "Hot Peppers", it was in the middle of the rectangular square. A big, menacing-looking bodyguard frisked us before letting us in. Inside it was quite big, there was a U-shaped stage in the middle, surrounded by tables and chairs. The place was dimly lit and there were half naked girls, possibly a little older than myself, dancing on the stage and walking through the tables.

What I was left with that night, was that awkward feeling, that uneasy discomfort, which you can choose to ignore but cannot deny. Your brain perceives there's something terribly unnatural in the air and it defends you from it, trying to steer you away.

Of course sooner or later the unescapably and wonderfully human condition, condition of weakness, subsides this feeling, but still, the conflict between your morality and *humanity* persists, no matter how long ago it has been forgotten.

Chapter 8

Valor

The goliardic and adventurous feeling slowly died. But in its place was left the satisfaction of living in a place where things mattered and what I did was necessary. I felt happy, and I was no longer depressed and weak. Every morning I would wake up earlier than I had ever gotten up before, and think "today I shall strive to live". And every night I would collapse on my bed, knowing I had fulfilled my goal.

Still, there were ins and outs. I never regretted not being able to live with the *finer* things in life, actually I enjoyed the stepdown in my lifestyle. But it took some time to come to grips with the reality of what I had done, and the dark nature in the place I had found. Up until then I had lived being treated with silk gloves and seeing things from a position of privilege. People had of course *taught* me about the *bad* things in life. But their teachings were worthless because they had no more knowledge in the matter than I did. There is a very clear line between words and truth, words can be heard, forgotten, disregarded. Truth can only be acquired and experienced, and it scars you in bad and well.

One day, casually, I caught an earlier bus to the construction site and got there before everyone else. The gate was open and there was a car parked outside so I went in. As I passed the office building, I saw the boss and another man carrying a black bag. It was long and they were each holding an end of it. The only possible explanation that could be given to this, immediately terrorized me. They threw the bag into the *foundations* of the building, which later that day would be covered in cement. I slowly turned around, and exited the construction site, praying they wouldn't see me. They didn't. I never told anyone about this and I went to work that day as if nothing had happened. I talked and laughed, and did my best to ignore what I had seen. But I couldn't forget it no matter how hard I tried, and I couldn't fight off the irresistible urge to do something to try and fix whatever evil I had discovered. Back when I lacked nothing in my life, I did as I pleased; I had everything to lose and I, effectively, could lose nothing. But now I had stumbled upon the need for pragmatism. There was nothing I could do, and I was locked inside something I had never thought would trouble me: the impossibility to satisfy my will. But the spirit and the fire inside, knew no pragmatism.

In time, I thought, in *time*.

The next couple of months were relatively unimportant. Life went on and I cherished every single day of it. As I became more self-sufficient, the memory of my past life and my parents, faded away and lost significance. I did feel sorry for them, I couldn't deny that my disappearance must have caused them much anguish, but I didn't regret it. I knew my time to do something with my life was limited, and staying in that place would have determined my destiny for the rest of my days. Sometimes I thought of the future, and what would happen to me when I was forty or so. I knew I wouldn't be a construction worker forever. But I figured I would cross that bridge when it came. The future was sure to bring unexpected and wonderful things, serendipity. For now, all that mattered was making each day count. Feeling happy each day, living with no regrets, not one. Every day had a routine to it, but every day was fundamentally different. Every night at the Tigra we would meet different people, with different stories and different backgrounds. And every day my fascination with the world grew to a transcendent height. Life went on, and time flew by. But this time I was not looking at it flying away from me, I myself was flying in the sky on the *verge of eternity*. It was a happy time.

I enjoyed the daily chores and tasks. I humbled myself enough to go down to the mission church and get some new clothes. The woman in charge saw I had nothing to put the clothes in, so she was kind enough to give me a backpack. I cut a deal with the girl at the front desk of my hotel and she gave me a monthly rate. Based on my calculations, I could save enough money to last for a while. We were paid in cash each week, no receipt. I stashed my cash in my room behind the radiator. Mickey kindly offered to let me sleep on the sofa at his place, but I declined saying that I appreciated the gesture. Truth was I enjoyed living on my own, and as long as I could afford it, while still making good economics, there was no reason to move out. After all the years of living in my father's house, where everything reminded me of my family and what I came from, it was a nice break to have my own place. A place where I didn't need to feel like a stranger. It was mine, I had earned the right to live there and no one could tell me to leave. Only I had that choice to make.

I took pleasure in coming home to *my* apartment, going out for walks, clearing my head and just being alone with my thoughts.

When you break life down, it all comes to a few moments which determine what you will accomplish and what kind of a person you will be. How we live these so significant moments of our lives, is precisely the choice we must make. Those months in Prague where perhaps the most significant in my life. From the ingenuous boy I was slowly forged into a man, and a human being, wiser in the ways of the world and the knowledge of himself. Every evening, before meeting with my friends, I would walk down to the Moldava and cross the St Charles Bridge. I would smoke a cigarette as I watched the sunset and gazed into the last reddish light in the sky. The smoke from my cigarette would blend with the view and resemble a dark cloud a few inches from my eyes. Then the smoke would dissolve in the air, and the sun would set, and I would go to the Tigra to have dinner.

The city slowly became familiar, I could never say it turned into my home, but it did have something comforting in it. It started to grow on me and the more time went by, the more I found in Prague a place where I could feel safe. I had no need to hide or run. I was slowly becoming lazy and letting the sedentary, average life have the best of me. But deep down, I knew I wasn't ready to set camp in one place, I knew I would never be able to subdue my desire to explore the world and face my fears.

It was a Friday evening, we were having dinner at the Tigra, as usual. We drank and ate like there was no end to our stomach and our liver. By now we knew most of the regulars, so people kept stopping at our table to have a beer and merrily waste their time with us. In the Tigra there were no barriers between people. You would talk to anyone like they were your best friend, and everyone was affected by the same, binding, good humour. I left a little earlier than the others since I was working Saturdays as well, to make ends meet. I would say it was fairly late when I stepped out onto the cold street. It was raining lightly so I tightened my overcoat, the same one I had arrived in, except now it looked a little less classy and a little more lived-in. I light a cigarette. I had pawned my cigarette case for the money, but I kept my lighter. It was gold so I could have made quite a bit off it, but it had too much sentimental value. It was something from my past life. It had always been like a lucky charm, a light, really. And unfortunately for me, a memory, more than anything else.

I was going home so I could get a decent good night sleep, and ease the following day's work. I decided to take a detour to walk off all the beer with some fresh air and exercise. The alcohol oxidized well and left me with a nice, calm state of mind.

I was about halfway home when I heard a scream. It was more of a shriek, like a desperate cry for help. I froze in my tracks while processing the sound, which was not very easy because of all the alcohol in my system. Another scream woke me out of my trance and I sprang into action.

I ran towards the cry. It was leading me behind the small park with the playground that I had passed on my first day in the city.

Following the sound and my instincts, I found myself in the parking lot of the playground. It was an underpass, dark and wet. I could only see the silhouettes of three men and a victim, a girl. Two of the men were holding her arms in place while the other was standing in front of her, his hands on her body.

Then I yelled something insignificant at the top of my lungs, trying to sound more confident than I was. I must have been successful since the man in front of the girl turned around in a startle. For a split second there was a moment of awkwardness in which he didn't say anything and I remained still, not knowing what to do next. He said something in Czech to the other two and came towards me. They had been drinking, I could tell from the distinctive smell and the quantity of glass bottles on the ground next to a minivan, the only car in the parking lot which I assumed was theirs. He skipped the "go away or I'll beat you up" talk and hit me on the jaw straight up. The punch was powerful but imprecise, hitting with only one knuckle, the rest bouncing off onto my neck. Next he flung his body at me in a football tackle. The whole thing had happened in a split second and I hadn't had time to react. He was pushing me with energy while he yelled, and I heard him in the background. I quickly backtracked until I landed on the railing of the lot. I hit my back on the pole but didn't feel the pain. Concentrating on my footing, I found the strength and the technique to rotate my hips and throw him to the ground using my arms. I jumped on him before he had time to get up. The struggle had made me angry beyond control and I was eager to punish him, so I hit him as hard as I could, repeatedly. One after another, I landed infinite punches on his face. Each one was like a chisel, chipping away at the immense block of anger inside me. Blood was coming out of his mouth and nose, his eyes were dark-purple and closed. The other two attackers let the girl go and came towards me. I could not see them since I was focused on my prey. Lifting my head, I had just enough time to glimpse a glass bottle crash onto my forehead. I blacked out for only a few seconds but it was enough. When I opened my eyes I had my back against the railing, and I could taste and smell blood, all over my face. The first man was in front of me, his face bloodier than mine. He smiled when I opened my eyes. It was a mean smile, wry and eager for vengeance. He charged his arms backwards and was about to hit me with a crowbar. My body was in pain, but my soul grew stronger with every hit I took. It pushed me to go further and gave me focus and conviction.

I saw him load the strike and prepared my reaction, covering my face with my elbows. When he made impact I pivoted my right forearm on the other side of the metal bar and ripped it out of his grip. As quickly as I could, I grabbed it with my hands and hit him straight on the temple. I hit swiftly, leaving the bar on him for less than a second so he wouldn't have time to grab it. The other two tried to attack me but I menacingly waved the bar at them, backtracking in my steps so I could have a clear view of all three. They looked at each other, then turned around, hurried to their car and sped out of the lot.

I dropped the metal bar on the pavement, and my knees quickly followed. Barely breathing. My face was covered in blood and my body was drenched in sweat. When I was able to stand I thought of how glad I was they had left. I could not resist the urge of being relieved. But I was more than that, I was impressed with myself for doing something right, and surprised at the power of will I had managed to muster. And I felt strong.

I looked around for the girl but she was nowhere in sight. A little disappointed, I started walking out of the parking lot when I heard a muffled sob coming from the darkness. I stopped, trying to process the sound, again, slowly, but because of the beating this time, not the alcohol. I went towards the corner of the parking lot and kneeled down in front of the crouched figure.

I made some reassuring comments and accepted the requirement for some senseless conversation before she muttered a few words and I could say, "Come with me, you must trust me."

She stepped out of the darkness and a stray beam of streetlight illuminated her face. I was shocked at the sight.

It was Ashley.

Chapter 9

Farther into the Fray

That was it. No goodbyes, thanks, farewells. I just left. Prague was over. The devil of chance had caught up with me and brought it all back. I had a vivid memory of everything I had tried to forget in the past couple of months. I hated it, seeing myself as the person I used to be. But I could live with it. I knew it was part of me whether I liked it or not and I could not wave it off like *a bad dream*. I couldn't choose my past, but I could choose what kind of a person that past would turn me into. What kind of a person I'd be in the future. A person who has no past is worthless and empty. A person who has a profound knowledge of their past, regardless of what it may be, is blessed by the gift of truth, and can see through the aberrations of his society.

If I were to live in denial then, I could never hope to have a peaceful life and meet my true goals, since I couldn't possibly know them, as I wouldn't know myself.

Leaving Prague was, rationally speaking, a mistake. It showed weakness and fear on my part. I couldn't bare confronting Ashley and mixing the two worlds I had lived in. The simple idea, was like a glimpse at a horrifying scene, which I was not yet ready to take in. It was hard for me to run away, again. I had given up all the progress I had accomplished in a matter of minutes, the time it took me to decide to leave my first act as a man, a coward. The physical pain I experienced was nothing next to the excruciating thoughts on my pitiful conduct. I convinced myself that the woman I had saved that night only had a vague resemblance to Ashley and I was mistaken. In the end I stopped believing in either theory and resigned, doubting the entire event hadn't been a product of my imagination. Once again I was completely and utterly lost. A few minutes later, I thought of the friends I had made in Prague, and the friends I had left behind in Rome, how *similar* they were, and I started crying.

The departure was much like the first time. No planned destination, no contact, not much of a reason to leave. It just felt good to travel, and take on the world head first, to be dynamic. Alone towards the unknown.

The money I had stashed away would get me pretty far, so I wasn't particularly worried about that. Besides, by now I had no problem living on a margin. After a while your stomach gets used to bad food and skipping meals. Hunger is a state of mind, like many other things it was induced by habit and my definition of normality. If I could manage to stop feeling sorry for myself and thinking of food, then I could beat it. There was something profoundly meaningful in averting the most *normal* of desires, and hunger was a good starting point.

The clothes I had were sufficient to keep me warm and comfortable.

I felt bad about not being able to say goodbye to the friends I had made, not saying goodbye to that city, which had taken me in a very peculiar moment of my life.

I found myself thinking of the time I had spent in Prague, while I was on a train going towards Kaliningrad. Why Kaliningrad?

I bought a map of Europe at a tobacco store and Kaliningrad was the first place I looked at, defying chance. The train had left the station at six am, so I had had just enough time to go back to the hotel, pack my stuff, settle the bill, have a few beers as I waited until morning, and walk to the station. I went into a deep sleep the moment I settled down into my seat, courtesy of the graciously altering Czech beer.

I woke up somewhere around Warsaw. The countryside was even more rundown than the one near Prague. We passed several abandoned stations along the way. They were old constructions built with cheap materials during the USSR period, and then never used again, except by the homeless. The devastation of the past.

The train shook as it changed tracks, just as it had on the morning I had arrived in Prague. The coach was more than half-empty, and the people onboard were sleeping silently. I enjoyed the quiet ride.

I got to Kaliningrad in midafternoon. The sky was grey and the clouds were fairly low. The station area was bleak and inhospitable. The temperature was slightly colder than Prague. I smoked a cigarette on the quay and then went inside to gather some information. Finding a couple of coupons, I set my mind on a nice place near the harbor, and left the station. Walking in the city center was like walking in time. It felt like post World War Two soviet-block. The buildings were all in that same style, and all had that frightening totalitarian impression about them. As I got to the area near Konigsberg dome, the architecture turned to different time periods, prior to the soviet era. This part of the city had an indescribable character, something beyond art. The scattered vegetation along the quiet streets, and the red bricks of the imposingly beautiful dome, and the dark wood shutters on the windows of the buildings. The fresh sea air that swept through the street in a gush of wind, as I got closer to the harbor.

The port was visibly very old. You could feel it as you passed by the docks, and the nearby factory buildings. The places where people from a different time had lived and died, and fought for their dreams, such as *labor laws*. History had taken its course, things had happened, lives had changed. It seemed normal to picture it in one's mind. The breezy air and the distant horizon, scattered with only a few ships, inspired the illusion of freedom in me once more. I breathed in heavily and enjoyed the freshness, as I walked along the quay. The hotel was located in the old part of the harbor village. The reception was fairly nice and tastefully decorated in a maritime style, lots of wooden furniture, paintings of storms on the walls, and there was a model of an ocean liner placed on a coffee table in the middle of the lobby. The clerk asked me what room I wanted. Trying to be polite, but get my message across, I said whichever was cheapest. She smiled at me, and said she would give me one with an ocean view for the same price as the others. I felt like I was in heaven for receiving such a kindness and thanked her sincerely. The room was small and nothing fancy, but it maintained the same style from the lobby, and the cracks in the walls matched the ones in my head. There was a nice view of the port and the sea beyond, from a small balcony. This place was costing me a little more than what I could have gotten in other areas in town, but I was fully content of my choice, and couldn't have felt better. It was late when I got to the room. I considered going out, but changed my mind as I looked at the comfortable bed, and thought of the joy of not having to wake up the following morning.

I slept well into the next day, and when I got up I felt the most relaxed I had in ages. I drew the curtains and squinted at the light. It didn't take long for my eyes to adjust since the sun was being filtered by the many clouds in the sky. The harbor was in full operation. Some workers unloaded crates and moved merchandise from ships to a warehouse and vice versa. The sea was calm and the ships stayed still. Their rusty hulls unmoved by the gentle waves. A light sprinkle of rain came down from the sky and froze the earth below. I opened the doors to the balcony and shivered at the touch of the cold breeze against my bare skin. Ignoring the cold, I inhaled deeply as I smoked a cigarette and looked at the ships. Afterwards, I had a warm shower and decided to go out for some breakfast. In the end I skipped breakfast and had lunch instead. The food was typically East European, filling, tasty and cheap. After lunch I went to visit Konigsberg Dome and happened to stumble upon a small enclosure outside the Dome containing only Kant's grave. Oddly enough I had been studying him in school before I had fled Rome. Not that I had paid attention in class, but there was something less boring, in fact deeply intriguing, about being around the real thing and not just some words on a page. In the enclosure, within that uselessly short steel gate, I could feel the presence of something I had not yet appreciated about the German philosopher. It was like being vividly reminded of something I had learned long ago, farther and farther back in time. Something I had always chosen to defy, and I still chose so. The brutal sensation of weakness and imminent peril I witnessed in front of the stone grave, is something utterly unshakable, for the words chiseled on that slab of marble will persecute me forever.

"Two things awe me most: the starry heavens above me and the moral law within me. I do not seek or conjecture either of them as if they were veiled obscurities or extravagances beyond the horizon of my vision; I see them before me and connect them immediately with the consciousness of my existence."

Immanuel Kant.

The reason why these words frightened me was because they intrinsically convey a command to elevate our nature by subduing our attachment to material aspirations. Although I recognized myself in this latent begrudging of the tangible, I was determined to strive within the world I despised. I was running not out of pure disinterestedness, rather I was deeply interested in changing what I saw as rancid and poisonous. I was travelling to find the one thing necessary: a domineering will. Not a domineering sense of morality as Kant would have had it.

I spent the rest of the day walking along the piers of the harbor. The ships came and left, forcing the seagulls out of the way when they passed. So they would fly up in the air only to return a few minutes later and continue their incessant fishing. The sun slowly lowered itself and the streets went dimmer, the vivid red of the brick walls faded a few shades. And the sky, the sky was a heterogeneous mix of light-blue, then white, yellow, orange and progressively darker shades of red drowning into the sea. The stillness in the air was seldom interrupted by the flight of a bird, or the shout of a seaman, longing to finish his working day. I smoked and took in the scene, not wanting to say a word.

Before long, the grey shadow of darkness arose over my head, and slowly turned into the dead of night. I always had wanted to watch an entire sunset; I'd never gotten the chance I guess. It fell in-between dinner and getting ready to go out. I realized then, how many things I had overlooked, when I was caught up in my lively circle. I used to think I was busy; I didn't have time. It became clear to me then that time was relative, and there was no measure by human means. There were only myself, and the tangible world before my eyes. *The latter made me feel weak and impotent, as if my importance were reduced to the nothingness of my surroundings; the former I felt as something independent and characteristic to my personality, and in it I saw the completion of my nature.*

I decided to walk through the neighborhood, in search of a good pub before turning in.

I found one after about twenty minutes of directionless wandering. It looked quiet and original. It was small, mal kept and rough around the edges. There were a few men that I recognized as workers from the docks. They were sitting at a booth in the corner drinking beer and chatting quietly. No tourists.

I sat down at the bar and asked for a beer in Russian, the concierge from the hotel had taught me how. As the bartender poured the beer for me, I thought of how much money I had been spending and how much I had left. I still had quite a bit of money, certainly enough for a while, but for the last couple of days I had been treating myself to a good hotel and decent meals. I wanted to move, after a couple of more good night sleeps. But moving would cost me, so I knew that the next destination would be cheap, and the accommodations unfavorable. I sipped the lager slowly, and watched the images on the TV.

A man entered the bar. He looked like he was in his mid-forties, but he seemed more like a bad-looking thirty-year-old than a good-looking fifty-year-old. The bags under his eyes and the scattered gray hair on his head, symptoms of stress, not old age. He was wearing a suit, which was strange considering the kind of pub. He had on a gold watch, his haircut was stylish, though you could tell it had been neglected lately, and his suit was a dark blue pinstripe with a red tie. Everything about his outside appearance indicated prestige and wealth. But as a human being, he looked tired, bored and almost depressed.

When he sat down he contemplated the moment for a while. He seemed out of place. Still, there was something about him, a certain quality, security, in the way he moved around and used his body language. A certain energy he'd radiated when he'd walked into the room. The bartender looked at him unsure of what to do. Daring not to disturb him. Finally, the man lifted his head and ordered a beer. I was sitting a few stools down from him.

"Why are you here?" he said in my direction. His voice sounded familiar, as if I had been hearing it for years.

I looked at him at loss for words.

"Why are you here? The only people who go on vacation this time of year are either old or rich."

He was implying I was poor, which bothered me for a slight second, then I remembered I was no longer rich.

"You're lost, aren't you? I can see it in your eyes.

"And I know."

He looked away from me and stared into space, or time, remembering something from his past.

"You mustn't feel lost. It's only a way of living in denial."

"You're looking for something I can see that, only you don't know what it is, do you?"

So many words wanted to part my lips, I couldn't express myself.

"There's nothing you can find here, only far away. You must experience the *poetry* of solitude. But you can never be alone in your world, the world that has seen you grow, that has shaped you and twisted your very definition of truth. And you must abandon your pain.

"I'll see you in a lifetime, junior

"Oh, remember, it's not about what you must find, it's about the truth you must confront."

He left the bar, I hadn't said a single word and his beer glass lay on the counter untouched.

I took it as I had already finished mine and I figured he wasn't coming back. When I lifted his glass to bring it to my mouth I realized instead of a coaster, beneath it lay a book. It was small and old

La prose du Transiberian was the name of the book and Blaise Cendrars the author. I opened it and skimmed the verses. Could this be the poetry of solitude of which the man had been talking? I was a little confused. How did he know I spoke French? How did he know so many things about me to pick at the frays of my open wounds with such accuracy?

Something out of a dream.

I took the book home with me and read it in about half an hour before going to bed.

The bizarre, incomprehensible, futuristic poetry, put order in my mind.

I would get on the Trans-Siberian train in Moscow and head for the east.

Chapter 10

Far and Away

I went to the docks and asked around for transportation to Moscow. It took a while before I found someone willing to help me. Partly because there weren't many people on the docks altogether, it was around 5 am, I hadn't slept all night.

An old fisherman, who was getting ready to go out to sea, told me the best way to get into Russia was by ship through St Petersburg; but they had cancelled the ferry service years ago, so I would have to see about it some other way. I thanked him for his time, and he got on his boat and set off. The sky was slowly turning from a very light-blue to a golden yellow as the sun rose into the day. I killed some time in a bar near the harbor, the only one open, and had a full breakfast. As I settled the bill, I asked the host if he knew of any ships going to St Petersburg. He told me to ask someone at the harbor, not showing any particular interest. I walked along the quay and went towards the big ships. The side my hotel was closest to, was the smaller side of the harbor, with all of the fishing boats and whatnot. On the far side, the one closest to the sea, were the ships. Freighters mostly, a couple of tankers too. The freighters were my best chance.

I was standing about a hundred yards from the ship. I could feel my heart pumping the blood into my veins and I felt nervous, knowing even if my life depended on it, I wanted to get on that ship. I tossed my cigarette and went towards the man with the clipboard. He appeared to be the captain, even though he wasn't wearing a uniform of any sort. He was balding on the head and had a long, dark-red beard which covered part of his face and was shaped by the blowing wind. The other half of his face was wrinkled around the edges, and tanned by the sun and the sea air.

He finished giving orders to the crew and looked at me. There was a brief second during which neither of us said anything. Then he felt his pockets for what I assumed was a cigarette and I offered him one of mine.

"What do you want?" he said taking the smoke.

"I need to get to St Petersburg, I'll do any work necessary to repay for the journey and I wouldn't cause any inconvenience."

"I'm sorry, I can't take you," he answered quickly.

"I promise you, you wouldn't even notice me.

"Please," I had nothing to lose.

"Why do you want to go to St Petersburg?"

I tried to find something to say, a somewhat reasonable explanation, but came up with nothing.

"Alright get on board, but I don't want to see you ever again. I have never seen you." He swallowed hard. "When we get to the port, get off as soon as possible, before the customs officials get on board, after that you're on your own."

"Thank you."

He looked at me and nodded as he exhaled, then he turned his back and walked away. Getting on board was easy, no one asked any questions. They spoke rarely amongst each other as they worked. A few of them looked at me, the others didn't bother to lift their heads. Either too tired or simply indifferent.

The ship sailed and left the harbor with a loud whistle of the horn. All the scene was missing was a bunch of people on the docks waving their hands. Nonetheless I admired the skyline of Kaliningrad and silently bade my farewell.

The trip was not very long but it felt like an eternity. I stayed on the stern of the vessel where no one came, and quietly enjoyed my free ride as I endured the cold. The air was freezing, but pure and rich of that indescribable scent the sea has. We sailed all day and all night. I never left the stern of the boat, not wanting to transgress the captain's orders. The man had felt me and become instantly familiar, making contact with my soul, or whatever it is which makes you feel powerless and strong at the same time. And I was grateful.

That was the night I discovered the gift of hope. I never would have thought I could find such an affable person in a total stranger. And I realized how familiar and understanding, a nice person could be.

The night sky took over, and the day came to an end. Covered by the stars and drowned in the cold, I appreciated my solitude and tranquillity, turning the place into a safe haven, protected from the overwhelming mass of water around. For the time being, on that boat, I was distant and detached from the suction of the land I had finally parted with.

But as the ship sailed in, I felt confident and knew I was a man, capable of living, *and not living in vain.*

Getting into St Petersburg was easy. I minded my own business and left the port. My heart didn't skip a single beat as I walked past the security checkpoint like a *ghost*. Nervousness and anxiety were a thing of the past. The fear which had once dictated my life, was no longer there. I had already accepted my past as a part of myself and taken whatever lesson I could from it. Now I accepted my present and found faith and hope, in my ability to confront the world, whatever it may prove to be. Growing stronger with every fall I might encounter.

I found the bus station easily. By now I had gotten used to stopping people on the street, asking them for directions, and orienting myself in an unknown city. When I got to the desk I was informed there wouldn't be a bus to Moscow until the next day. The news was disappointing but not discouraging. After all, I wasn't confined to a time schedule or any sort of obligation. The rest of the day went something like the ones I had passed in Kaliningrad, and I was thrilled by the challenge of yet another new city, farther and farther away.

I spent some time in a park reading the poem the strange man had left on the bar, a few times, accumulating desire and anticipation for my next adventure. I imagined what I would do, and dreamed of how much more I would evolve, through time and experience, and *sufferance*. It started to rain in the late afternoon. I went into a restaurant and had a few beers as I looked outside the window. The rain kept pouring from the sky, incessantly, and came down onto the empty city. I saw only a few passers-by, hurrying to a shelter and off the grey streets of St Petersburg. A few customers came in for dinner. They looked like they came from money, judging from the way they were dressed and the way they summoned the waiter. One of them was rude in his ways and he laughed a lot, the other was more temperate and inspired responsibility and privileged standing. They had salmon, fresh from the North Sea. I had goulash. I felt sorry for them, I don't know why, I just did. It was the first time I had ever felt any empathy towards another human being. How *weak* I have been, I thought. I was studying them intently with my eyes, but my vision went far beyond their physical appearance, seeing in them a different nuance of myself, and the people I had known.

Around eleven o'clock, I had been in the restaurant for a very long time. The owner told me he was ready to close up and I had to leave, so I settled the bill, and slipped the waiter a tip as I shook his hand on my way out. The storm had wound down and was spitting its last drops of rain. I walked without a destination, tired of plans and security, tired of fear, and tired in general.

It was cold, but I was dressed heavily and filled with food, and felt well enough. Getting out of the central area of town, I saw an old construction site. Probably one of the ones the soviet regime had started with great ambition, but then dropped halfway through, either for lack of funds, or for lack of spirit. The structure had been completed, and there was a roof that could protect me from the weather. It was my best option so far, and I was drunk enough to fall into a wonderful sleep. I went inside, no locked door or fence, no barrier to protect me from the outside. In the middle of the ground floor, there were some small mountains of garbage and a few old mattresses. I lay down on a mattress and closed my eyes, hoping I would be safe. A few minutes later a sound caught my attention. It had come from upstairs and it was something like a can falling to the ground. Unable to ignore it, I got up and looked around. There was a staircase on the far wall of the structure. I went towards it, making as little noise as I could. I climbed up the stairs and stepped onto the second floor, there was nothing but a deathly silence and a very ominous atmosphere. Listening intently, I heard the faint crackle of a fire. As I walked along the wall I saw the light coming from behind the next corner. The fire had been lit in an old trashcan, and radiated light and heat in the air. An old man was standing in front of it, his hands above the flame. Seeing this, reminded me of how cold and wet I was. The man turned towards me. He said something in Russian and looked at me, waiting for an answer, as if he had been expecting me. He was apparently harmless and didn't seem contrary to the idea of sharing his fire. As I got closer to him I realized there was something very odd about the old man. If indeed he was old, I had assumed he was elderly, but frankly I couldn't see much of his face at all. He had a large hat on his head, which fell well below his eyes. His beard and his hair were unkempt and dirty to the point you could not tell what color they were. But the strangest thing about him was his clothes. His clothes seemed to me as if they had been extremely expensive and well-designed, sometime in the distant past. But they had been ruined by bad weather and constant use. They had holes on the elbows and the knees, and there was a hole on the back of the coat, about the height of the right shoulder blade. It was small and well-defined, unlike those caused by time, this one had been caused by a precise strike. Perhaps a bullet. As I got within feet from him, his face looked familiar, though it was still impossible to distinguish the features, underneath the hair, the wrinkles and the hat.

For a second I thought of leaving, but my curiosity and my stupidity outweighed my fear.

"Come here, young man," he said. Deducing I didn't speak Russian, I assumed.

"Bad weather." His voice was a little high-pitched, the tone was ironic and preaching. I was a little alienated by the situation, and I nodded silently.

"When I was young; I was very different from what I am now," he volunteered.

He talked to me for a long time, narrating his life story and lessons, what he planned to do, his philosophy of life. I listened subconsciously as I faded into a deep sleep. The last words I heard, before I passed out, were:

"We only express our true state of bliss, when we are most… *In danger.*"

The next morning there was no sign of him. In fact, I doubted the whole thing had actually happened, and I hadn't just dreamed it. I was confused to the point of doubting the existence of the man, had I not distracted myself with the notion I had a bus to catch, I think I would have ended in doubting my own existence.

The bus left in the afternoon, which gave me ample time to walk to the station and stop somewhere to get something to eat. The girl at the desk, the day before, had been kind enough to warn me that there was no meal plan, and the bus drove straight for about a full day. When I got to the station, I went to the office to buy my ticket and say hello to the girl. She gave me the ticket, I said goodbye and thanked her for telling me to bring food for the trip. I liked her. She was pretty, but unassuming. Unpretentious and wholesome, humble and true. A girl I hardly knew, and I would never see again, yet it was in her that I found and saw that feeling.

The bus wasn't as shabby as I would have expected from the low price of the ticket. It had comfortable seats and a small individual TV, which I was glad to ignore, as I did with the food I had brought. All I did on the ride was look outside the window, at the people working and living in the Russian countryside. They farmed the lands near their homes, which would have been much nicer before the highway was built. I was fascinated and shocked by the size of the real world. The one I hadn't seen up until a few months before, and perhaps would never see entirely.

All these people, everyone around me, they all had their lives, children, wives, problems. Who was I in this vast Vortex? What made me special and different from everyone else?

My mind tormented me with questions, as I dazed into a trance.

The bus was about half-full. Mostly with young business men, who traveled for work but couldn't afford to make the commute by train. They wore cheap suits and had old briefcases, most of them spent hours looking at their documents and scribbling away on their notebooks. They frowned, looking professional and *experienced*, at pieces of paper. Few times did they look up to see or do something else. They were too caught up in their chaotic world of stress and responsibility. I would have liked to baffle them, and show them how stress-free and happy I was. But I couldn't, for some reason, I was starting to feel all the pain I was running away from. The reality of things was closing in on me, and everything I was doing to prevent it was turning into a climax of pain.

We arrived in Moscow at around 7 am the next morning. I felt relaxed and well rested. Another violent change in my state of mind had worked its magic, and I felt great.

I thought of staying for a few days to visit the town, but I couldn't spare the money. On top of that I was desperately eager to start my new adventure towards the farthest place from home I had ever been. That is, if indeed I had ever had a home, really.

I walked hurriedly through the town, heading for the station. My heart raced with anticipation and I felt more excited than I had in years. The thrill of being alone, travelling and leaving my culture behind, but taking my *heritage* with me. I was ready to renounce to everything I had ever known, and reach for the other side of the Caucasian divide. Beyond that train station there was no turning back. In some ways, there was no origin, and truly no destination, and I was, dynamically, caught in the midst of my *cataphracted* existence. There was nothing within me that would give me the consciousness of what I would find or do, it was all just a fading, deepening darkness. And I raced towards it, falling further still into my dreamlike adventure, my spirit higher than ever.

When I got to the ticket office, I paid for the cheapest ticket available, I wanted to travel, and not see the world from a first-class ticket. With time I gave up all of the prejudices that had been instilled in me as a child, and discovered my own truth, my own life.

The train left early that Sunday morning. I got on only a few minutes before it pulled out of the station with a loud whistle and left the western world behind. Magic.

Chapter 11

Il Milione

Every second was a discovery, a revelation. Every image seemed oddly familiar, but somehow different and original in all ways. The train was ordinary. Something like the ones I had taken up until then. But in this one, I didn't pay much attention to the people on it, or the train itself. It was unimportant to me. It was only an instrument, to get to the other side of the world. An instrument that would allow me to find myself and break through the mystery and uncertainty that had clogged up my vision, all my life. A metal tube to pierce through the wilderness and unfavorable territory outside and reach for, the *final destination*.

I stayed in my seat for ours at a time, rarely getting up to stretch my legs or get something to eat. I just sat there, looking outside and contemplating my existence. The emptiness of the deserted land made me feel more alone with every day that passed. And gave me the final release of every turmoil, destroying it, which had influenced my past. The future, however, was still fascinating and mysterious. But the confidence in me, led me to believe that I would always be able to count on what no one could touch and only I possessed, that which lay within. However my life would unravel, I would always make my own choices and they would be the ones I would forever consider as right. Because I knew that there was something, deep down, which defined me as a person. And I would learn, and never cease to be impressed and to change with joy everything about me, when my judgment would see fit. But the essence, the substance, within would forever be my guiding light and my compass, my legacy.

That's why I had never been able to fall into any category. I had never considered myself part of a group. I had never managed to pretend I was an anonymous member of a society of which I used to be afraid and now I saw clearly, in all its pettiness and mendaciousness.

Whatever I may become in the future, I knew that I could never bend myself to the accommodations of the mass and fall into the Vortex. I would forever be my own reference point and give myself my own guidance, through whatever destiny I chose.

And it felt right, honest and true. The only truth I had ever known. And the only honesty I knew was the honesty with myself.

I wondered what was happening to the world I had left behind. How they would react if they knew what I had done, what I planned to do, the person I had become. The train blew through the countryside, through days of nonstop travel. Enough to drive someone insane, making him obsess on the distance from the *final destination*.

The train stopped for a day in the north of Kazakhstan. I got out, leaving that coach for the first time in four days. The station was very much unlike the ones in Europe. The platform was in the open air, surrounded by the wilderness. The town was smaller than any village I had ever been to. No more than five-hundred inhabitants, mostly old but a few children as well. The adults must have been working in other parts of the country, or maybe they had fled entirely, in search of a better life. Still though, it was unusually beautiful, the rural village surrounded by wilderness. It seemed like something I would have imagined, back when I was in so much pain, to escape and seek protection.

The only restaurant in town was the home of a local. The conductor of the train had set me in the right direction and I found it easily. I walked in the door and a woman of about forty years of age, though it is difficult to tell in these situations, greeted me with a smile, showing me to a table in the corner. Although we did not speak the same language, we understood each other just fine, and I realized human interaction and communication went beyond words and languages. In fact, I finally admitted to myself how limiting and superficial the language capacities I had always prided myself upon were, as opposed to everything which could not be put into prose but existed nonetheless.

The other passengers had stayed on the train, seeking the protection and silver lining they expected from the world. A couple of them even gave me an odd look as they saw me getting off. The food was decent and the meal was humble, and the restaurant was characteristic and agreeable. After lunch, I paid in Russian rubles and digested the meal while I walked around the dirt roads of the small town. I saw a few kids playing soccer in a field. The snow, the cold weather, and their poverty, didn't stand in the way of them having fun and smiling at me as I passed by. Beyond the field, the town ended and began the wild vegetation. The train station was on the opposite side of the village. I walked into the wild, minding my step as I made my way through. The terrain was partially covered in snow. The frozen grass below, crackled as I stepped on it. A few of the last leaves parted the trees as the wind blew, and fell onto my head. The sun shone through a few clouds and hit my face, making me cover my eyes with my hand. And I looked down at the shiny snow, which reflected the light and resembled a diamond carpet. The forest became less dense as I reached a clearing with a lake in the middle. It was frozen on the edges and still in the centre. The cold water mirrored the sky in its magnificent stillness and colour. The golden lake, a pool of inner strength, I thought to myself. I sat down on the edge of the forest and listened to the silence and the animals within. When the sun started receding, I headed back to the train to spend the night. Backtracking in my steps, I passed through the small town once more, and made eye contact with the villagers; they smiled at me and nodded, sharing with me all of their humanity and their hope. It was indeed very strange, that such an apparently insignificant episode of my life could have had such importance and meaning, but it did. And it went beyond the episode, beyond the actual village, which became an idea, more than anything else.

The lost Village in Kazakhstan had given me my most valuable life lesson yet.

Even in the most desolate land I had seen and met human beings like myself. In my most lonely hours I had found human contact. It seemed evident to me then, that there was nothing *noble,* or even convenient, about living in a circle and estranging the parts of reality far from my own. Because humanity is beautiful and human contact was the only thing that could ever matter, then.

We made one other stop before Vladivostok. The train blew its whistle, breaking the early morning silence. I lifted my head from the back of my seat. Still half asleep, I was soon told we were on the eastern border of Mongolia, and would be leaving again later in the afternoon. I looked out the window at the plains. The scenery was very different from Kazakhstan. There wasn't a tree in sight, only desert. I got off the train and breathed in deeply. The air was light and rare in oxygen, because of the altitude; the vanishing flatness, frightful. The pure emptiness appalled me, beyond imagination. Not a single soul, not a single living thing for miles in the distance. The place was free and untouched by the vulgarity of man. And it had nothing in it but primordial nature. The order of the beginnings, before the contamination of our civilization. It was beautiful and true, nonetheless devastatingly empty. Being there made me think of what that desolate land missed; people. Human beings to live in it and respect it, and leave their heritage and legacy behind. But origins are important. They would necessarily serve as refuge to me. Appreciating the untouched and empty, was difficult for a person who used to love people as much as I did. But I now saw the beginnings as a reference point, something to gauge and appreciate the beauty of honest civilizations, such as the village in Kazakhstan, where the people lived their lives in hard work and honest emotions. But equally that pure emptiness would gauge the aberrations and distortions of any world which spiraled out of human contempt. And as devastating as necessary, as powerful as required, the beginnings would always rule my judgment and push me to destroy whatever creation lay beneath them. Every creation worth as little as next to nothing, or as much as transcendence, is one step above primordiality. It must necessarily rest on human contact, and it is driven by our indomitable will, the strongest thing *in* nature. Any other foundation, any other twisted and contrived society, will, one day or another, perish and start over again. This is what I am, this is what I plan to do. This is what it truly means to be entitled.

No more fear.

Chapter 12

Living in Danger

The train arrived in Vladivostok a couple of weeks after it had left from Moscow. I got off and consciously set foot on the land of the Far East. Getting used to not living on a train took a while. It had only been a couple of weeks since the hotel in Kaliningrad, but it seemed like a *lifetime*. I felt like an entirely different person, the air smelled better, for once the sky was finite and less frightening, and my eyes were sharper and vision clearer. I still didn't have all the moves figured out, but I no longer was afraid of the future. And I was convinced society would never forge me, I would forge society.

I slept under bridges and underpasses, met people, most of them good and some of them bad. I avoided physical contact but didn't shy away from it when self-defense was necessary, and I felt the healthy urge to risk my life.

Every day I made the same choice. I chose I wanted to live dangerously, but live all the same, and throw away every prejudice I used to have, so I could embrace the world as I saw it. It wasn't easy at first, but with time the concrete pavement on which I slept grew more comfortable. And the stale bread which I would get, cheaply, from restaurants and supermarkets, tasted better. And I felt strong, stronger than I ever had been.

Instead of reminiscing my past and wishing for the comfort in life I used to have, I thought of the very beginnings of my own person and my European culture. The beauty and viciousness of the longest, most significant history the world had ever known. And I thought of the people who had left their legacy on that history, on time itself.

I decided I wanted to somehow leave a legacy behind as well. But where should I start? How could I possibly change *my* world? And how could I change the world for other people, more or less *enlightened* than myself? Maybe just a bunch of Byronic nonsense to some, but illuminations to me. In time I would return to society with the power of the truth I had found at the end of the tunnel of youth, and apply it to everything I had left behind. With all my resources and all my strength, and all the conviction in the world, based on the belief in what I saw as true and honest and worth changing in society. The means, whatever they were, I would come up with later on. For now, I focused on building my character and laying the foundations for my shrewd morality as a human being. I was convinced, I would be able to handle anything coming my way, and overcome it with grace and the will to start over and fight when the time came. If the timing was right I had no idea, but I wanted to fight and unleash myself against the *evils* of the world. Whether it was juvenile goliardy or clarity of vision, I'll never know. But I knew that to express myself and set something right, to leave a legacy behind; I needed to live *in danger.*

When I got word of a demonstration which would take place in Beijing, against the totalitarian communist party, I didn't think twice. I relished at the idea of protesting and screaming in the crowd, showing off all of my anger. So I used up what was close to the remainder of my savings to get a train ticket for Beijing. Worth it, I thought.

It felt like embarking on a mission, an adventure. The train moved quickly, alongside the North Korean border. One of the last forbidden countries in the world. I toyed with the idea of smuggling myself in, but dismissed it for lack of a plan. But if the chance had arisen, I probably would have done it.

I'm not ashamed to say, I had found something deeply intriguing in danger, and the subversion of human sentiments, such as fear. I guess it was indeed naïve of me to try and fight my humanity, but that doesn't mean it was wrong. If I had to define that desire for immortality and eternal youth, I would say it was most truthful way of expressing myself in *that* moment of my life.

The countryside was entirely different from Europe, as was everything else, mostly. The vegetation was bright green, trees were short and the mountains were *young*, their summits sharper. The sun was shining on the crops and farmhouses. The closer we got to Beijing, the bleaker it became. The sun became blocked by thick clouds of smoke, polluting the clean sky. The greenery shrunk until it faded completely before my eyes, and the farmhouses were now shooting skyscrapers.

I got off the train and stepped into my dream. I could hear my heart beat, louder and louder as I ran through the crowd. Running through the tunnel, to *the final destination*. And, for a few seconds, I finally became that man I had always wanted to be. I stepped into that legacy.

I opened my eyes a few days later in a hospital bed. The doctors informed me I was recovering from a bullet wound to the right shoulder blade. My ideal of immortality was crushed, along with my dreams of eternal youth. I got the sensation there was an ominous presence nearby, someone I knew that, deep down, I was *afraid* to face. Philip Randen entered the room. I closed my eyes and thought about everything that had happened to me, since the last time we had met, in the garage, so long ago. I looked at my godfather and studied him. He was wearing a three-piece suit and was as elegant as usual. As *elegant* as I had been, when I was a part of his distorted world. He took off his leather gloves and held them in his left hand. His appearance made a spot of wealth and power, in contrast with the poverty of that so-called hospital. I expected him to come towards me and shake my hand, but he just stood there instead, grazing the rabbit skin interior of the gloves with his right index finger.

"Hello, Max," he said.

"Philip." I nodded at him, without giving him the satisfaction of any emotion.

"Aren't you surprised to see me?" he said, after a while.

Here it comes, I thought.

"What was it, Philip? How did you find me? The hospital records?"

"Yes."

We were playing a game, whoever showed any weakness first would lose. I knew I wouldn't lose, I was a grown man now, with the strength to confront anything life brought. And I was ready to go back home, to Rome. What I would end up doing was still an epic question mark. But I knew it would be extraordinary and in one way or another, I would create a legacy to leave behind.

"Why, Max?"

"Why not? Would you have wanted me to spin my wheels, toying with the pose of the noble, respectable millionaire?" I took a deep breath.

Philip just looked at me, waiting for me to finish, probably preparing his rebuttal like a good lawyer, I thought.

"It's madness, Philip. Madness," I said looking into his eyes, reaching for that honesty I knew was somewhere inside of him.

"I know," he said, looking down and blushing. It was the first time I had ever seen him lose his stoical stance. I had won the game, but I didn't feel as expected. Even though I had forever severed my ties to that world, I still had something to lose. I still had to reach for the long-lost humanity at the bottom of it,

I still carried that debt. Looking at my godfather, I realized that there was still something clean, something useful, left in my hometown. And it would be noble to seek it.

"I am glad to see you, you know," I said.

"Thanks, me too.

"I admire you, Max, you're a very courageous man, you'll be a very successful person, and, I dare say, a much wiser... *human being*, than I ever was."

"I appreciate it. Thanks, Philip."

In those few seconds, I was rewarded by that gift for hope, it seemed clear now. All this time, I had been searching for something, running away or running towards, when I realized that what I had been looking for could be found even in the darkest corners of the world, even in the madness I had left behind. Because if I wanted to live well and die well, if necessary, I was to live in hope.

"Philip? Where are my parents?"

He shifted position and breathed in deeply, visibly disturbed by the question.

"Your parents are dead, Max.

"I guess they weren't as strong as you..."

His words trailed off as he left his sentence in mid-air, or maybe I stopped listening. Not wanting the dream to become nightmare.

For a brief time back then, I thought that nothing could make me feel emotional, nothing could pull me downwards. That I was beyond emotion, and I was stronger. But the news of the death of my parents, changed everything. So they did love me, after all. They were my beginnings, my reference point.

And emotion is a wonderful thing. Because it makes us human, even *fear*. The art of emotion lies in channelling and selecting it, perfecting and ultimating your humanity. Whatever destiny you may discover, or forge for yourself, your humanity will guide you through life, and it will persist long after you are dead, because transcendence and legacy are one and the same.

And it is the only thing that truly requires a search to be found.

It is not a search on the outside, but an infinite quest we are all confined to, which plunders to the bottom of our transcendental nature.

Now I saw it clearly, this goliardic dream, spurred by the gravity of my solitude and the cataphraction of my loneliness. But all I had were a lot of elusive phrases and picturesque memories, which lacked the very strength I had hoped to achieve.

Even in the euphoria of youth we are human, and we only grasp our condition when we are most... *in danger.*

Chapter 13

Eternally, I

It's five-thirty am. I have an alarm set for six but I've been awake for over an hour. My eyes have been opening and closing the whole night. I look at the ceiling for a while and think of my past, trying to find something in it that may be of help. But I know that whatever happens I'll be able to do the right thing. I think of everything that had been done and said since the beginning of my venture. How I had staked my entire fortune to try and bring some decency to the financial world. How I had fought for the interest of my clients and everything I had found along the way. All the integrity, all the good intentions, and all the lives that I had managed to change. And I thought of the end, most likely very close. How I had been misled and set off course, how naïve I had been to trust certain people, but how right I had been in attempting to make that desperate leap of faith and fully trust another human being. But in the end I had lost. I knew that. It was over, everything I had built would be destroyed in the near future, sold, mortgaged, loaned. I had the power to stop it, but at the cost of the jobs and houses of thousands of average people. I could save myself, but saving my firm I would forever define me as a human being. I would never be able to erase the consequences of my actions. I knew what the right thing to do was, and I knew I had the strength in me to do it. The cost was irrelevant and the damage didn't matter because in the end, I knew, eventually, I would reach the destiny I had always been meant for, ever since I was a boy. I would start over from nothing a thousand times if I had to, but each time I would keep the moral stubbornness that had brought me down the time before. And the criticism and hate I would get didn't scare me, they would be gasoline and wood to aliment the youthful fire I, so jealously, had maintained all these years. Because it had nothing to do with age, or time. The only thing I was afraid of was becoming someone else, and stepping out of my cataphraction, by breaking the indivisible I, which lay at the bottom of my existence. And once I made the decision to flee the vortex, that decision would change me forever, *finding myself* lost in the grief and sorrow for the life I had left behind.

My actions had always defined me as a person because they had always been backed with all of my strength and my integrity, which came pretty close to being enough. And today as well I would enter that conference room proud, standing tall with my head just as high on the last day as it had been on the first. No regrets. And I'll start over, continually, until I manage to reflect my personality into this world I so intimately despise. To impose my ideas, my values, my leadership. I will create my legacy and leave when a domineering will is established. Whether I find it in the battle, or inside my armor, I shall find it, and restore; peace.

I got up and turned off the alarm. I walked around the room in a daze, then went to the bathroom. I opened the door and turned on the glaring light of the cheap luxury hotel. I took one of the single serving soap tubes and rinsed my hands under the tepid water. I took a shower and tended my personal hygiene for a full hour, as if I were getting married instead of going to my last conference as the chairman of my own company. I did my best to hide the bags under my eyes and pulled whatever grey hairs I could find. Afterwards I put on a blue pinstripe, three-piece suit with a red tie and a gold watch, and went down to the lobby of the hotel to have breakfast. My business partner George had already gotten a table and was studying some documents.

"Hey," I said.

"Hey, listen to me!" he said with excitement.

"I've been working all night and I think if we merge with the Russians we might be able to pull through."

"What makes you think they'll go for it?" I said, indulging him, even though I knew I would never become a partner of the Russian firm with which we were meeting later on.

"They're in the same situation we are. The thing is they're not going to give us capital because they need it themselves. But if we merge and combine our assets, we can cover each other," he said, his eyes sparkling, his hands trembling and his lips quivering from the exhaustion and the coffee.

"Look. We can't do it," I deliberated.

"Why not?" he shot back.

"Because you know better than I do that the only thing those guys are good at is firing people!" And that was not the reason, I couldn't express it then and I cannot now, but if you are attentive, and as committed to life as I am, you can see it perfectly.

"So what! This is the game we chose to play—"

"No. There's no game, there never was. I'm sorry, George.

"You don't know how much. I don't expect you to understand this, but I owe it to myself to take the fall for this one.

"What we're going to do is go there, ask them for capital, which they probably won't give us, say goodbye and figure out the next move on our own."

"Which is??"

"I don't know. Probably we'll liquidate as long as we can stay afloat and then file for bankruptcy."

He said nothing and we both just looked outside at the rainy streets of Kaliningrad, suffering. But at least I suffered with the hope that there was something valuable in doing what I was about to do, that someday, every piece of the puzzle would fit in and my legacy would be complete.

"The end justifies the means," he said. I smiled at the quote.

"Macchiavelli," I said.

It was always comforting to be able to refer to one of our idols, as a shield. In that moment I could have quoted every single man I had idolized on the topic of ethics, and reply to George. But I didn't feel strongly enough to say anything, so I remained silent. Then I suddenly changed my mind

"I think, George, the time may have come, to step out of the Renaissance..."

He said nothing.

"Come on, George, follow me in, after that I can't force you to stand behind me. I trust you to do what you see as right."

We hadn't eaten anything and we left the buffet with upset stomachs. I ignored my body and rested all faith in my soul, finding the strength and guidance to face my fear.

We stood outside the building, hesitating to go in.

"Want a cigarette?" George said, handing me the pack.

I thought for a second and then said, "No, thanks."

"You sure?"

"Yeah, we've wasted enough time. Let's go in."

Before entering the conference room on the 20th floor of the tallest building in town, George and I went to the bathroom. As we were washing our hands, we made eye contact in the mirror. He was afraid, I could feel it. He clung onto the only material assets he knew, fearing anything else and greatest of all was the fear of falling. I looked into his eyes and kept a straight face, knowing that the fall was an ally and the only thing that counted was the will to act, and get back up, starting from the *beginnings*.

The meeting with the Russians went even worse than I had expected. The main guy was a sly fellow. He stood on a pedestal and presumed from up top. Looking down on us, not touching anyone, except through his leather gloves. Once in a while he took them off, and caressed the inside with his right index finger. Intimidating, is how I would have defined him a while *ago*, but now all I *see is* presumption and a big fall from it. They refused financing right away and started pushing for a merger. In the midst of the verbal vomit flowing out of the room I heard:

"We stand strong, do what we have to do, the storm will pass eventually, and people like us will still be afloat."

After a while George changed sides on me and started favouring the Russians. I got up, apologized, and left the room.

As I'm leaving George catches up with me.

"Max, if we don't do this, we're alone. We have no one else. It's this or nothing. Don't you get it! No one will help us."

I stop and turn towards him, looking into his fearful eyes and thinking of what to say. I take a deep breath and tell him something I should have realized myself long ago.

"Solitude is painful. But the love of pain, and the love of suffering, is the love of an ideal for which to suffer, and most of all the love of life itself.

"I'm sorry to bring you down with me, George. But trust me, some day, you and I, we're going to sum it all up and we're going to ask ourselves *what was it all for?*

"Today the answer is nothing. And until that changes, *I suffer*.

"But not today. Not today."

In this negation, I woke to my *cataphracted* condition as a human, and overcame its eternal pain, the challenging acceptance of our humanity. And driver of the youthful quest, which, evidently, had no relation to age, but was the definition of my existence, and to which I could not escape, as a Human...

But I now have the strength to take off the masque, the armor, the façade, and *face* fear itself, no battle, No pain.

Only the love of life.

Because to love life is not a choice nor duty. It was the sentence we were given in order to exist, what we must see as the limit to our nihilist spirit.

The impossible negation.

"Only a God can save us now."

Martin Heidegger.

Author's Note

Max's story is the exemplification of all that is honest and true in youth. He comes into a world where the odds of him being able to find himself, and not see that fear of anonymity, become a reality, are and always will be, against him. But ultimately, his illumination, *the cataphraction* of his existence, will lead him to the end of the tunnel of youth. Where he will find his own guidance, and the ability to guide his potential reality, to the transcendence of his legacy.

But the concept of youth, as outlaid in the book, goes beyond the goliardic and Byronic subversion of life, which is a characteristic of the adolescence of all human beings. The concept of youth, is to be viewed as that moment between the beginning of a being's existence, and the incorporation of this being into the *accommodations of the mass*, with subsequent loss of his ability to find a higher meaning to his life, as he becomes a part of a system, which does not define him. Youth is that moment of resistance and strenuous fight against the system. And, more often than not, this moment of *cataphraction* and resistance, leads to a further loss of oneself. But if the search is proficient, and the pain endured, there is the possibility of finding that higher meaning, and the conquest of the truth as to one's own position in the universe. Once this is achieved, one becomes a *negationist,* which means he negates and disavows the influence of the mass on his fate, and its judgment on his legacy. But Max goes beyond even that, he reaches the *maximum* degree of negationism, and becomes a God, surpassing the limits we all share for he and his story pertain to the realm of idea.

That is why you cannot see him, even though he can see you, in all your potential realities; and, ultimately, he does not exist. But if you are patient and your desire is strong enough, you can find him, anywhere, anyhow. Ambition, is the only requirement. And through the dramatic realization of hope, idea and reality merge into our own prerogative to *the future.* We *are* the future for it lives within us and outside of us in our aspirations and our projects, it is the conniving laziness which permeates the critical thought of the 21st century which impedes us from living it and impedes *us* from flight.

There are no answers in "The Human God", nor is there anything noble in having the presumption to know them.

There is the triumph of legacy over time, sustained by an inwards leap of faith, and the unconditional negation of everything else. The grasp for the transcendent truth, which goes beyond the time dimension, and is glimpsed through the cataphracted existence of the outlier, and possessed by the *negationist;* who stands and negates its torture. Which is the sentence to love the transcendent idea of life in a world which is finite and ended towards sufferance.

But why do we suffer?

The reason why we suffer, is because we are condemned to love an idea we cannot possess, we are condemned to accept our limits

"The starry heavens above me, and the moral law within me."

Immanuel Kant

In any case, although it is unavoidable, we must not fear. Whether we go beyond even the metaphysical or not take one step outside of ourselves is irrelevant, for it is when we close our eyes that we can clearly see that singularity which is the proof of our existence.

Alas, it is fully true that we all, at some point in our lives, would like to go back, but we cannot. And we must choose to go forwards.

Yes, this is a tale of rage, passion, truth and love, and yes this is the story of our generation. And *yes* it is imperative that we go forwards, because

"A *concealed* YES drives us that is stronger than all our NO'S. Our strength itself will no longer endure us in the old decaying soil: we venture away, we venture *ourselves:* the world is still rich and undiscovered, and even to perish is better than to become half-hearted and poisonous. Our strength itself drives us to sea, where all suns have hitherto gone down: we know of a new world."

Friedrich Nietzsche (The Will to Power section 405)

A consistent way of thinking for the post-contemporary dilemma, and a radical measure for the make benefit of a lost society.

I dedicate this book to all "Highly Effective teens" and other people who have the courage to call themselves extraordinary.

We'll see each other in the light of the unstoppable future we believe in, and *our* great dream will finally cease to elude us once we are all *Human Gods*...

Tancredi Lyle Rapone.